A Christmas WEDDING

Featuring

A *Groom* for CHRISTMAS

&

A *Bride* for CHRISTMAS

Michelynn Christy

Published by Blessed Publishing
Cover design by *iCreate Designs*
Formatting by Polgarus Studio

ISBN: 978-1-940492-32-2
10 9 8 7 6 5 4 3 2 1

For my Bridegroom
I am my Beloved's, and my Beloved is mine

A

Groom

FOR

CHRISTMAS

(formerly *A Christmas to Remember*)

Michelynn Christy

Published by Blessed Publishing
Cover design by *iCreate Designs*
Formatting by Polgarus Studio

CHAPTER ONE

I can't believe I'm doing this! Samantha frantically ran the brush through her hair. There were a bazillion things she needed to pack before heading out to Mom's. Clothing, toiletries, camera, and the gifts. The gifts - the ones she hadn't even purchased yet!

Of course, why would she have needed to purchase gifts if she hadn't planned on returning home for Christmas? No, this was not the plan. The plan was to spend an exciting Christmas weekend with Tammy and Jill. And that *had* been the plan until yesterday. Why couldn't her roommates have informed her sooner that they were going home for Christmas? But the brink of Christmas Eve? Well, that was just fine and dandy! It was a wonderful plan for them – they were sisters. They had each other. What would she do now? Spend Christmas all alone? Not gonna happen.

A quick phone call to Mom and a new plan had been forged. Of course, now she'd have to pay triple for the airfare. And purchase gifts. *There goes my spring break.* Oh well, it was Christmas. And she was determined to make it a memorable one.

"Ma'am, would you like a blanket or pillow?"

Samantha glanced up at the flight attendant. "Both would be great. Thanks."

She gladly took the items from the flight attendant's hands and immediately wrapped the blanket around her. Maybe a nap would relieve some of her anxiety.

This would be her first time home since she'd left for college nearly a year and a half ago. Leaving home had been rough. And if she were honest with herself, deep inside she really didn't even want to go away to college. But she had to. She had to get away from *him.*

Travis.

He'd first asked her out for a date in high school. They'd met at a football game. He was rooting for the opposing team, so she assumed he attended their rival school. She'd been correct. He was a couple of years older and way out of her league, she'd thought.

Dating Travis would be a dream come true – and it was. They went out nearly every weekend and spent most of their free time together. Anyone could clearly see that she and Travis were in love. Many nights they'd talked about a future together. She often dreamt of the day she'd become his wife. He was all she'd ever wanted – handsome, thoughtful, caring, or so she'd thought.

I don't understand what went wrong. Even now, she fought back tears. Perhaps it wouldn't have been so bad if she hadn't given herself away to him. She'd always planned on waiting till marriage, of finding that perfect one. She was so sure they'd be married someday. He'd said he loved her.

He'd lied. And she'd been naïve enough to believe his words.

Everything was wonderful until a couple of months after graduation. That's when she got the dreaded text message. He wanted to break up. He thought it would be a good idea if they dated other people. Why would she want to date anyone else when she'd already found her perfect match?

Stinkin' liar. How could someone just throw

away a two-year relationship? The coward could have at least broken up with her in person. But then he'd have to look her in the eye. He'd have to see the hurt on her face and the pain he'd caused.

She quickly brushed away the tear that slid down her cheek unbidden. Why was this still so difficult? It wasn't because he was good-looking, or because he had plenty of money. No, she was certain it was because she'd loved him with all her heart. She'd believed he was her soul mate – the one person in this world she was to cherish all her days. She'd given him *everything*, believing he was reciprocating her affections. But instead of her anticipated marriage proposal, Travis had dumped her like yesterday's garbage.

An ostentatious chortle brought her attention to a young man just beyond the empty seat beside her. His face was bright as he stared at the airline catalog in his hands. He glanced her way and noticed she'd been watching. How couldn't she? Chances are, all the passengers heard his jovial outburst.

"You've got to see this!" He handed the catalog to Samantha.

She glanced down at the advertisement and smiled. The front of the t-shirt for sale read 'Let's eat

Grandma!' other than 'Let's eat, Grandma!'; the back read 'Punctuation saves lives'. She recalled seeing something like that on Facebook before, but apparently this was the first time this man had seen it.

Samantha nodded. "It's funny." She handed the catalog back to him.

"Sorry, if I bothered you." His forehead creased.

"Oh no, it's fine." A change of thought was welcoming.

The young man held out his hand. "My name's William."

She reluctantly shook his hand. She'd never been too keen on meeting strangers. "Samantha."

"Where're you going?" he asked.

Should she share her plans with a complete stranger? She eyed him covertly. By his jeans, raglan shirt, and baseball cap, she figured he was just a friendly all-American guy. She guessed him to be about twenty-five. "Fresno," she divulged. It wasn't *exactly* her destination, but that's the airport she'd be arriving at.

"Really? Me too. Do you have family there?"

"Yes. Well, not *in* Fresno. My parents live in a small town, not too far from there. How about you?"

"All my family's back East. I really hated to leave them right before the holidays, but my new employer called and requested that I come early. I guess they had an emergency and wanted me to help out."

"Where will you be working?"

"At a church. I'm their new youth pastor."

"Oh."

"Not your typical job, I know. But serving the youth is my passion. It's such a dynamic age – just between childhood and adulthood. It's a difficult time for many of them and I want to show them God's love and help them make wise decisions that can have a positive impact on the rest of their lives."

Yep, he was certainly excited about his new career.

A voice called over the intercom. "Please return to your seats and fasten your safety belts. We will be arriving in Fresno in approximately thirty minutes."

Samantha noticed a few passengers heading back to their seats.

"Do you attend church anywhere?" He grinned.

Samantha shook her head. "No."

"Well, if you're looking for a place to attend, you'll already know the youth pastor." He chuckled.

"I don't know if you'd consider that a positive or a negative."

She smiled. This guy didn't seem anything like how she'd envisioned a pastor.

"Ooh, no response. That's never a good sign."

"No, it's just that...you're not anything like what I'd imagined a pastor to be."

He winced. "Is that a good thing or a bad thing?"

"Good, I think."

He wrote down an address and phone number on the back of a little booklet and handed it to her. "We'll be having a candlelight service at a quarter to midnight on Christmas Eve. You're welcome to join us."

She received the invitation from his hand and slipped it into her purse. "Thank you."

"So, do you have big plans for Christmas?"

"I've got dinner at my parents' house on Christmas Eve. The following morning, my extended relatives will come over for breakfast and we'll exchange gifts." In spite of the unpleasant memories of Travis, she was glad to be home. Truthfully, there was no place she'd rather be. "How about you?"

"Not quite sure. I'm staying with the pastor and his wife. He's an older gentleman, so I don't think they have any children at home. I don't know how they usually celebrate the holidays. I have a feeling that they won't be doing too much, though. Part of the reason I'm starting my job early is because Pastor Marshall sprained his ankle. He has to wear a cast on his entire leg for at least six weeks."

"Oh no, that's terrible. Does that mean you'll be preaching?"

He chuckled. "I hope not. The congregation might just get up and leave, if I did."

"But I thought–"

"I'm just the youth pastor. I don't mind being in front of a group of young folks, but looking out at adults scares me to death. We had to preach before a congregation several times in Bible College. That's when I determined I'm more comfortable with young people." He smiled. "I have to keep reminding myself of the verse 'For God hath not given us a spirit of fear...'"

"What will you be doing at the church then?"

"I imagine I'll be driving Pastor Marshall around to make his usual visits. And I'll help out wherever I'm needed." He shrugged.

"Even if it means preaching?" She raised a brow.

"If they ask me to, I will. But I'm hoping they

won't ask. They have an assistant pastor and I'm guessing he fills in when needed."

"I hate public speaking too."

This time, the pilot's voice spoke. "Flight crew, prepare for landing."

"It looks like we're about to arrive. Well, Samantha, it was a pleasure meeting you." He smiled. "Hopefully, we'll see each other again sometime."

"It was nice meeting you too." Was it really time to go? A part of her wished she could have more time to get to know William. He was so friendly and easy to talk to.

CHAPTER TWO

Samantha took a deep breath and knocked on the door. Wouldn't Mom be surprised she'd found a ride home from the airport? As it turned out, William was headed to Kingsburg as well. The assistant pastor had been sent to pick William up and offered her a ride. Samantha gratefully accepted. There was no need for Mom to drive all that way when she already had transportation.

She noticed Mom had purchased a beautiful new Christmas wreath for the front door. The usual lights and decorations were displayed on the lawn and Samantha looked forward to this evening when she could see the town decorated with lights.

"Samantha?" Jamie smiled as she opened the door.

She immediately threw her arms around her

sister. How good it was to be home! Other than Mom, Jamie had been her favorite person in the world growing up. And even though Jamie was three years older, they'd remained close friends throughout their high school years. She'd worked extra hard in her child development studies and graduated from Fresno State early. No doubt, she'd already been offered a position at one of the leading preschools in the valley.

"How's school?" Jamie inquired.

Samantha grimaced. "You don't want to know."

Jamie laughed. "That bad, huh? You never did care much for school. I was surprised you decided to go off to college."

Of all the things she'd shared with her sister, her immense heartbreak had not been one of them. While Jamie had always worn her emotions on her sleeve; Samantha often concealed hers and bore her burdens alone in silence. Neither was Jamie privy to Travis and Samantha's prior intimate relationship.

"I needed a change of scenery." Samantha noticed the house was unusually quiet. "Where are Mom and Dad?"

"I'm sure Dad's rummaging through the basement again, looking for more Christmas lights.

Mom had to run to the store to pick up some cranberry sauce for dinner tomorrow night."

"Is Scott coming?"

"I think so. He might even be bringing *somebody* with him." Jamie smiled.

"Somebody? As in, a *girlfriend*?" Samantha lifted a brow. Their older brother had always said he wanted to be a bachelor his whole life.

"Rumor has it."

Samantha shook her head, and then suddenly noticed a diamond ring on her sister's finger. Had it been there the whole time? Her mouth dropped open. "What's that?"

"A surprise."

"Really? I didn't even know you were dating anyone. You never said anything in your letters." She wrapped her sister in an embrace. "Oh, Jamie, congratulations! When do I get to meet him?"

"Tomorrow at dinner."

"I'm so happy for you."

"Me too." Jamie led the way down the hall. "Your room's all ready for you. I bet you're tired."

"I am, but I need to finish up some last-minute Christmas shopping. I hate to go to the mall this close to Christmas."

"It'll probably be better than River Park. It took me twenty minutes just to find a parking space last week."

"Do you think one of the malls in Visalia would be any better than Fresno?"

Jamie shook her head. "Probably not."

"Do you want to come with me?" Her eyes pled silently.

"I can't. I promised Mom I'd help her make the pies for tomorrow. Sorry." Jamie grimaced.

Samantha shrugged. "That's okay." She needed to buy a gift for her sister anyway, so it was probably better if she didn't go. "Should I wait for Mom?"

"You know how long Mom takes sometimes, especially if she runs into someone she knows. The mall could be closed by the time she returns."

Samantha laughed. "You're right. May I take your car since Mom's isn't here?"

Jamie frowned. "It needs gas."

"I can put some in."

"Sure. The keys are on the wall rack near the door."

Samantha grinned. The same place the family's keys had been nearly her entire life. That's part of what she loved about being home; familiarity. "Thanks. I should be back by dinner if I don't get stuck in traffic."

Samantha glanced down at the shopping bags in her hand and mentally rattled off the gifts she'd purchased. Sweater and scarf for Mom – check. Summer sausage and gourmet cheese gift basket for Dad – check. Baseball cap and jersey for Scott – check. Slippers for Grandma and Grandpa – check. Necklace for Jamie – to be purchased. Should she pick up a little something for Scott's girlfriend and Jamie's fiancé? That would be the last of her purchases – and most of her money.

She entered the jewelry store and perused the 14 karat gold pendants in the glass case in front of her. 'Sisters by birth – Friends by choice' she read the message inside the heart-shaped charm. *Perfect.*

"Samantha?"

She looked to her right. "Uh, William, right?" She smiled.

"You remembered."

"Or should I say 'Pastor William'?"

He chuckled. "No. Please. William is just fine."

"I'm not going to ask you what you're doing at a jewelry store." She raised an eyebrow. Did he have a significant other?

"Oh. Pastor Marshall asked me to pick up the gift he'd purchased for his wife. Since he's been out of commission, he couldn't come himself."

"Is that the only reason you came all the way to the mall?"

"Pretty much. Thanks to my GPS, I didn't have any trouble finding it. Just a parking space." He scratched his head, and then glanced down at his watch. "I don't have to be back for a couple of hours. Would you like to join me for a bite to eat?"

The last thing she'd expected when coming to the mall was a lunch date with a cute guy. Her cheeks flushed. "Um, sure."

"I saw a small seafood restaurant across the street. Do you like fish?"

"I love it."

"Great."

"So, how'd your shopping trip go?" Mom asked.

Samantha thought of her lunch date with William and smiled. "Great."

"Hmm...didn't sound like a normal 'great' to me." Mom set her fork down and cast a sideways glance toward Samantha.

"You should ask her about William," Jamie teased.

Dad's brow raised. "William?"

"We're just friends. We met on the plane. He's the new youth pastor at Hope Baptist Church."

"You're dating a pastor?" Mom didn't conceal her surprise.

"Youth pastor. And we're not really dating. We're just friends."

"Mm...hmm." Jamie clearly didn't buy it, even if it was the truth.

The truth was, she enjoyed William's company and his friendship. Even if William *was* interested in her, she had no idea what type of physical contact, if any, to expect from a man of his caliber.

"Will you be seeing this 'William friend' again?" Dad asked.

"He invited me to church tomorrow night. I'm not sure if I'll go."

"We have dinner on Christmas Eve," Mom reminded.

"It's just before midnight, so it wouldn't interfere with dinner."

Mom nodded.

"Why not go?" Jamie asked.

Samantha shrugged. "I don't know. Is it wrong

to go to a church service just to see someone you know?"

"He invited you, didn't he?" Mom smiled. "Besides, I don't think the people at church will mind an extra attendee for a special service."

"We'll see."

CHAPTER THREE

Out of all the gifts she'd purchased, Samantha was most excited about Jamie's. Hopefully, her sister would like the necklace as much as she did. It was special. She'd always wanted to give her sister something to show how much she appreciated their friendship.

"Sa-man-tha!" Scott's voice called from the dining room. "Get in here before we all starve to death."

Was it seven already? She glanced in the mirror and finished applying her lipstick. "Coming!" She smoothed her sweater and looked at her outfit again. Would this be good enough for the service tonight? She'd have to be careful while eating dinner, so that she wouldn't spill anything on her favorite top. It was the perfect color green that brought out the same hue in her eyes. Travis had always said it was a good color for her. Perhaps William would appreciate it too.

She gathered her wrapped gifts and made a quick stop in the living room to place them under the Christmas tree. Fortunately, everyone else was occupied and wouldn't be privy to her good deeds.

"It's about time, Squirt." Scott had always affectionately called her that and she didn't mind it a bit. He stood up from the table as she entered the dining room and moved toward her.

Samantha smiled and offered her brother a hug. "Hi, Scott."

His fierce embrace nearly knocked the wind out of her. At six foot two, he towered over her by about nine inches. "I've missed you."

She laughed. "I can tell."

"Meet Michaela, my girlfriend." His grin broadened.

Samantha hugged her brother's sweetheart. "Nice to meet you. You must be something special to have wrapped this big guy around your finger."

Michaela shook her head. "Scott's been the best."

A chuckle came from the other end of the table. "He sure has her fooled."

Samantha spun around. She knew that voice very well. "Travis?"

"Surprise," he said.

Samantha stared at Jamie, whose hand was clasped in Travis'. Her mouth dropped open. "I don't understand. *Y-you two*...are engaged?"

Jamie nodded. Samantha sensed regret in her expression.

How could her sister betray her like this? Samantha's lip began to quiver. "I...I'm not hungry anymore." She ran from the dining area and through the living room, slamming the front door on her way outside. Why hadn't anyone told her? She wouldn't even have returned home if she'd known this. Spending Christmas alone would be better than seeing her sister with her ex-boyfriend.

"Samantha!"

She heard Travis' voice, but she kept walking. She was nearly to the end of the block when he'd caught up with her.

She swiped a tear from her cheek. No doubt, her mascara was now smeared. "Go away, Travis!"

He grasped her arm and spun her around. "No. Hear me out, please."

"Take your hand off me."

He did as told. "Listen, Samantha. I still love you."

She stared at him in confusion. "I don't understand."

His brown eyes drew her in. He stepped closer and stroked her cheek. "*You're* the one that I want," the words dripped from his lips like honey on its comb.

When he came near to kiss her, she immediately stepped back. This wasn't making any sense to her. "I thought you and my sister were engaged."

"I don't love your sister. Jamie and I are only getting married because we have to. I'd much rather be marrying you."

"What? What are you saying Travis? What do you mean by you 'have' to?"

"I'm saying I knocked her up – Jamie's pregnant."

She stared at Travis in disbelief. "You are the biggest loser I've ever known. My sister's expecting *your* baby and you're out here trying to *kiss* me? You're pathetic. And I feel sorry that my sister will be stuck with you all her days. She deserves better. Grow up, Travis." Samantha swiftly turned on her heel and hurried back toward the house.

"Samantha, wait!"

She ignored him and kept walking.

Travis jogged to catch up with her again. "Your parents don't know yet. Please don't say anything."

She nodded briefly, but spoke nothing. There were no words to express the hurt and anger she felt. She was now pretty much over the fact that she could never be with Travis again, but to think she'd have to see his face at every family gathering for the rest of her life – and at her sister's side – unnerved her.

When Samantha reached the house, she unwittingly made eye contact with her sister. Could Jamie read the disappointment in her eyes? Did she convey her pity?

Samantha returned to her bedroom and began packing her things into her suitcase. She couldn't stay in this house any longer – not with her traitorous sister here. As soon as possible, she'd return to college.

"You don't have to go," Jamie's voice echoed from the doorway.

"Yes, I do."

She stepped into the room and closed the door behind her. "Please stay through the holidays. Travis said I could move in with him for a few days."

"I'm sure he did," Samantha mumbled. "When are you going to tell Mom and Dad?"

Jamie frowned. "Travis told you?"

Samantha remained silent. She wouldn't tell her what else he'd said. *Idiot.*

"Probably after Christmas. I didn't want to put a damper on the holiday spirit."

"No, of course, not." She couldn't help her sarcastic tone.

"Listen, Samantha. I know you and Travis used to date, but..." She frowned and her voice quivered. "I'm really sorry." Was Jamie crying?

"I'm sure you are."

"I don't know what else I can say to you."

"Just leave me, please."

"Okay." Jamie walked to the door. "You should still go to that service tonight. William sounds like a nice guy."

"He's one hundred times better and more honorable than Travis will ever be," she snapped back.

"I'm sure he is."

When Samantha heard the door click behind her, she quickly locked the door. She thought of Jamie's words. Maybe she would go to the service tonight after all. Anything that could help take her mind off her troubles would be welcome. And she'd get to see William.

CHAPTER FOUR

Although no snow had fallen, the evening temperatures had dropped considerably. Samantha initially considered walking to the church, since it was just a few blocks away, but ultimately decided driving would be best.

She blew into her hands and rubbed them together, hoping to create a little friction. The car's heater wouldn't even have a chance to warm by the time she arrived at the church. Hopefully, it would be warm inside the building.

Samantha took a deep breath and stepped into the church foyer. She'd arrived a little early to find a good seat. Her eyes roamed the congregants in search of William, but she couldn't spot him anywhere. Perhaps he was in the main sanctuary.

Immediately, she noticed William up on the stage.

He was pushing a wheel chair with an older gentleman seated in it. Surely the man in the wheel chair was the pastor with whom William was staying.

William glanced toward the door and smiled and waved when he caught her eye. He briefly spoke to the pastor, and then quickly descended the steps to meet her.

"You made it." His smile was bright as he approached.

"I did."

The suit he wore brought out the rich deep blue hues in his irises. William was indeed a good-looking man.

"I've got to be up on stage until the pastor introduces me to the congregation, but after that, I'll need a place to sit. Will you save me a spot on your pew?"

Samantha smiled. "Sure. I was hoping I wouldn't have to sit alone."

"Great." He looked around at the empty pews and pointed to the second row toward the front. "Would you like to sit there?"

"That's fine."

He seemed to eye her apparel, and then met her gaze. "You look nice."

She was certain her cheeks turned three shades of scarlet. "Thank you. I wasn't sure what to wear, but I didn't want to freeze."

He nodded in understanding.

"You look good too. I mean, uh, blue is a great color for you. It really brings out your eyes."

"That's what my mom always said." He chuckled. "Seems she was right about a lot of things."

Had he worn the color just to impress *her*? She hoped so.

He led the way to their chosen pew. "I'll have to go back up on stage soon, so I can't sit here long."

"I understand."

"How was Christmas Eve dinner with your family?"

Samantha frowned. "I'd rather not talk about it."

"That bad, huh?"

"Worse."

"I'm sorry." He frowned. Was he genuinely concerned? "Well, hopefully tonight will be better."

"I'm counting on it."

William smiled and briefly squeezed her hand. "Good. Me too."

As soon as Pastor Marshall introduced William as the church's new youth pastor, to the congregation, they'd erupted in applause. Obviously, they were thrilled with their newest member. Perhaps they'd needed a youth pastor desperately.

William joined her, as promised, in the second pew.

A woman leaned over and shook William's hand. "Is this your wife?" She smiled at Samantha.

William cleared his throat. "Uh, no, just a friend."

Although the lady sent Samantha a knowing look, William's words bothered her. *Just a friend?* Is that all he considered her to be? She'd hoped she meant more than that to him. Perhaps, in her over-anticipation, she'd read his signals incorrectly.

She momentarily forgot about his words when the singing began. The stanzas of the Christmas carols were familiar to her, despite not growing up in church. She recognized most of the songs from hearing them on the radio over the years. They'd brought back fond memories of Christmases from her childhood years.

When a woman took the stage to perform a marvelous rendition of 'O Holy Night', Samantha was nearly brought to tears. It was the first time she'd ever heard the carol and she was certain the awe-inspiring words would be etched in her mind for all eternity. The song became alive as she pictured the babe in the manger and angels proclaiming Christ's birth. But for the life of her, she couldn't understand why that historical event was so significant. Maybe she would ask William later.

The assistant pastor gave a brief message and read Scriptures surrounding the event that happened over two thousand years ago. In conclusion, he asked the congregation a couple of questions. 'Do you personally know Jesus Christ, the Saviour of the world?' And, 'if you left this building this Christmas morning and were killed in a tragic accident, are you one hundred percent certain you'd go to Heaven?' The words struck Samantha's heart and shook her to the core. In all her life, she'd never contemplated those words.

When the pastor asked those who were unsure of their eternal destination to raise their hand, Samantha reluctantly did. Fortunately, everyone else's heads were bowed. She'd never cared for public recognition of any kind.

William glanced her way and smiled. He nodded, indicating that he'd like her to follow him. She did as he requested and the two of them stepped into the quiet foyer. He offered her a nearby chair to sit in.

"Why did you raise your hand?" He raised a brow.

Normally, she'd be reticent to speak what was on her heart. But for some inexplicable reason, William set her mind at ease. It was as though she'd be comfortable sharing anything and everything with him. "Because of what the pastor said. I don't know that I'd be in Heaven if I were to die."

"Do you want to know how you can be certain?"

"Yes, I do." She stared at him. "*Can* I be certain about something like that?"

"You can, according to the Bible. Would you like for me to show you?"

She nodded.

"Okay. First, let me ask you something. Have you ever done anything wrong?"

She laughed. "Yes, lots of things." She desperately hoped he wouldn't ask her *which* things she'd done. Although she was comfortable speaking with William, she didn't desire to scare this upright man away before they even had a chance at a relationship. What would he say if he knew about her and Travis?

"God's Word calls those things 'sin'. The Bible says 'sin is the transgression of the law', and it's something we've all done." He clasped his hands together. "But when Jesus came to earth all those years ago, something miraculous happened. He sacrificed His life for you and me. On our own, we could never be good enough to get to Heaven because the prerequisite is absolute perfection. Jesus Christ was the only One who could satisfy this holy requirement."

Samantha nodded in understanding.

"When we trust in Jesus, or maybe I should say, *believe* in Jesus, He steps into our place. When He died on the cross, He allowed God to place the sins of the whole world upon His back. He took the punishment for those sins – which was Hell – and then proved He was God by rising from the dead three days later. So, in effect, He paid the sin debt that you and I owed. This is a *gift* He freely offers to all mankind."

"So, what do *I* have to do to receive the gift?"

"The Bible says that 'If thou shalt confess with thy mouth the Lord Jesus, and shalt believe in thine heart that God hath raised him from the dead, thou shalt be saved. For with the heart man believeth unto righteousness; and with the mouth confession is made unto salvation.' And 'For whosoever shall call upon the name of the Lord shall be saved.'"

"So, that's it? All I have to do is believe from my heart and ask Him to save me?" Seriously?

"That's what God's Word says."

"What about helping old ladies cross the street and feeding the homeless?" Samantha heard the choir now singing in the auditorium.

William smiled. "Those are good things, no doubt. But the only thing necessary for salvation is believing in Jesus. Good works don't play a part in saving us. As a matter of fact, the Bible goes so far as to say that 'man is justified by faith *without* the deeds of the law'."

"So, how do I do this?"

"You can pray," he suggested.

"Okay. Is there anything special I need to say?"

He smiled. "No magic words required. Just talk to God from your heart."

Samantha smiled and bowed her head. "Dear Jesus," – she looked up – "is it okay to talk to Jesus, or should I say 'God'?"

"I don't think it matters. God is listening to your heart. I usually pray to God in Jesus' name."

She nodded and bowed her head again. "Dear God, in the name of Jesus, I ask you right now to save me. I believe from my heart and I'd like to go to Heaven. Amen. Thank you." She looked up at William. "Was that alright?"

"If it was from your heart, it was perfect." He grinned. "Shall we join the others?"

Samantha agreed and they entered the main sanctuary once again. The large room would be darkened if it weren't for the lit candles held by each participant. William summoned one of the ushers and he brought the two of them candles as well. William kindled his flame with the light from a man behind him and prompted Samantha to light hers. She brought her wick to William's flame and her candle caught fire.

Samantha looked around the auditorium and stood in awe at the beauty of the candlelight. There was something special about it all, something symbolic.

The pastor read a Scripture once again. "'I am the light of the world: he that followeth me shall not walk in darkness, but shall have the light of life.'"

William smiled at Samantha and she returned the sentiment. She closed her eyes and gave thanks that she now no longer walked in darkness. She now possessed The Light of Life.

CHAPTER FIVE

"What do folks usually do in these parts this time of the year?" William turned to Samantha. He took a sip of his hot cocoa and waited patiently as the church members greeted him.

"Most places are closed right now." She glanced into the darkness outside. "But we might be able to see the dancing lights."

His eyebrows shot up. "Dancing lights?"

"You'll understand when you see them. It's a decorated house out in the country. The owners put on a really cool light show. We can take my car if you'd like to go."

His warm gaze met hers. "I'd love to."

Samantha parked the car and tuned in the car radio

to the designated station. She and William watched as the bright Christmas lights 'danced' to the music playing.

"This is spectacular!"

"I told you it was cool," she teased.

"How long does it usually last?"

"I'm not sure, but I think there are like eight to ten songs. Do you want to stay for the whole show?"

"Sure. There's no place I'd rather be." His gaze lingered.

"Do you mean that?"

He nodded, and then slowly closed the gap between them. When his lips met hers, all Samantha's doubts about his feelings toward her flew out the window.

William's kiss was gentle, yet intense. But he quickly broke away. "I'm sorry. I shouldn't have done that."

Now she was confused. "Why not?"

"It was inappropriate." He shook his head. "I'm a youth pastor. What kind of example am I setting? If there's a member of the youth group in one of those cars, they could have seen me."

Samantha frowned. "Is there something wrong with kissing someone you care for?"

"Yes. I mean, no. Well, yes, if you're striving for purity."

"And you are?"

"Most definitely."

"So, what does that mean?"

"It means I should only kiss someone I plan to marry. Or better yet, only kiss the one who I will be married to."

"Oh." What would he think if he found out about her and Travis' prior relationship? Surely, he'd be appalled.

"That's not to mean that it won't be you. I just can't be sure yet. We only met the day before yesterday." He raked a hand through his hair. "Goodness, what was I thinking?"

"I don't know. But I know what *I* was thinking. I was thinking that you're a really great guy. You're kind, handsome, and I like you a lot. And you're a great kisser."

"Oh boy." He blew out a breath. "Samantha, I think you're wonderful too. I do care for you. However, you're going back to college in a couple of days and I'm staying here. I just don't see how this is going to work between us."

Samantha frowned. If he really did care, wouldn't

he find a way to make it work out between them? "You mean, you don't *want* it to work."

"No. That's *not* what I mean. All I'm saying is that if we continue this relationship, it will be very difficult for both of us. Long-distance relationships rarely work. I've seen it with guys in Bible college; either the girl or the guy meets someone else and the other one is left heartbroken."

She felt tears welling in her eyes. "So, that's it? You don't even want to *try* to make it work?"

"I'm going to leave that decision to you."

"What do *you* want?"

"Because of the situation, me just beginning this new position and you going back to college, I think maybe we should go our separate ways for now. And then, when you return home, if we both feel the same way, we can resume our relationship."

"You don't want to have any contact at all?"

"Samantha, I think you're misunderstanding me. I *do* care about you. A lot. I don't mind writing letters, phone calls, or any of that. I just think that it would drive me crazy to be dreaming about you, then find out later that you've been seeing someone else at college."

"I won't do that."

"Nobody *plans* to do it, sweetheart. It just happens."

"I don't have to go back to college. I could stay here with you." She knew she sounded desperate, but how could she lose a great guy like William? Good men were difficult to find.

"If you give up your dreams for me now, you'll resent me for it later. You've already made a commitment to go to college. Finish what you started. If it's God's will that we get back together, He will see to it that it happens." He gently moved a strand of hair from her face then lightly touched her cheek.

"Okay." So, this was it. This must be how nice guys break things off. "Does this mean that you'll date other girls while I'm gone?"

"I don't intend to. And I'm hoping that you won't see anybody else either; but if you do, I'll understand." He rubbed her arm. "Let's talk about something else, okay?"

She nodded.

"When do you leave?"

She'd thought about leaving tomorrow. "That depends."

"On what?"

"You."

"Well, I'd like to spend as much time with you as possible. I was hoping you could show me all around this little town."

That settled it. She could deal with her sister if it meant spending more time with William. "The second of January."

"Perfect. The only trouble I can foresee is telling you goodbye next year." He chuckled. "And abstaining from kissing you."

"That doesn't sound like a problem to me." She smiled. "I mean the kissing part – not the saying goodbye. I'd rather not discuss that."

"So, you won't have a problem not kissing me?" His brow raised.

"No. I don't see you kissing me as a problem."

"So, you like kissing."

"Very much so."

"Yep, that definitely could be a problem."

Samantha noticed the desire in his eyes. She suspected that, even now, he fought the urge to kiss her. "Okay, then let's have a no-kissing rule. I want to spend time with you without you worrying. So from now on, we won't even think about kissing."

William laughed. "If only it were that simple."

"Change of subject. Can you come over for breakfast this morning?" Thankfully, Jamie had said Travis wouldn't be there. It would be a good opportunity for her family to meet William.

"I'd love to."

CHAPTER SIX

Samantha pulled her comforter to her chin and stared up at the ceiling. Her eyes filled with unbidden tears that slid down her temples into her hairline, and eventually, her pillow. Why did females have to be so emotional anyway?

She thought of how her life had changed just in the few days since she'd met William. He was *so* different than any guy she'd ever known. Seriously, what guy doesn't want to drag you into the bed the first chance he gets? What kind of guy suggests not kissing until...until when? Marriage? Is that what William had meant?

If they abstained from any type of physical relationship, they'd probably get to know one another pretty well. If a man had no expectations in the physical realm, they would be free to bond in the emotional and spiritual realm. Something about all of it excited her. Yet, at the same time, she longed for his touch, his kiss.

Just the thought of spending time with this awesome man sent a thrill up her spine and shot right back down through her toes. If she could just hold on to something like this, to this relationship, it would be like living in a dream. William was so kind, so considerate. Yet, he was handsome and funny. And so so good.

Did she even deserve a guy like him? No, that was a question she would not dwell on. William had said that he felt like God brought them together. So, who was she to question God? A knock on her door forced her to wipe her tears away.

"Come in." She sat up.

"Hey, squirt." Scott popped his head through the door. "May I come in?"

Samantha patted a spot on her bed.

Her brother sat on the edge and his eyes met hers. "Wanna talk about it?"

She knew he was referring to what had happened on Christmas Eve. He must think it was the reason for her tears. "Not really."

His brow lowered. "Jaime's pretty torn up about what she did to you."

Samantha shrugged in silence. Actually, the situation with her sister was the *last* thing she wanted to think about right now. She had too many positive things to dwell on. Why would she want to entertain negative thoughts when she could think about William?

Scott knocked her knee with his shoulder. "Hey, how'd your date go? What was the guy's name? William?"

Samantha brightened. "William is wonderful!"

"Well, if he was able to lift you out of your fog, he must be something."

"He is." Her wistful smile quickly exchanged for an inquisitive brow. "You're a guy. Maybe you can answer a question for me."

He smiled. "That, I am. Shoot."

"What does it mean when a guy doesn't want to kiss you?"

Scott frowned. "Either he's gay or just wants to be friends."

Samantha smacked his arm. "He's not gay! He's a pastor!"

"Ow!" He rubbed his arm. "Well, you asked. That was the first thing that came to my mind. Sheesh! Forgive me, sis."

"Sorry. But I'm being serious. And he doesn't want to 'just be friends', he *did* kiss me." *Boy, did he.* She smiled.

"I don't think I understand your problem. He appeared pretty normal at breakfast yesterday." He shook his head. "Females are complicated."

"Guys. All they want is one thing, right?"

"Wait a minute. If you think I'm going to engage my little sister in a lesson about the birds and the bees–"

"Scott! Just answer my question."

"For the most part, yeah. But we're not *that* shallow."

"William's not like that. He wants to wait till he's married."

"You're already talking marriage? Look, Sam, you just met the guy. He seems really nice and all. In fact, I like him. But I don't think you're anywhere near the marriage stage."

"Scott!" She turned his head until he looked in her eyes. "I'm not talking about marrying William. At least, not right now. I'm just trying to figure him out. I mean, is he too good to be true?"

"I don't know. Do you want me to talk to him?"

"No."

"Well, you said he was a pastor, right? Do pastors take celibacy vows?"

"I don't think so. Most are married. He's not a priest or a monk. And he's talked about marriage. I think he just wants to wait."

"And you have a problem with that?"

"No."

Scott rubbed his forehead again. "What was this conversation about again?"

Samantha laughed. "Never mind, Scott. I think I got my answer."

"You did?" He smiled and shrugged. "Well, you know me. Scott, the answer man."

Samantha burst into laughter.

Scott rose from the bed and moved to the door. He turned, before stepping out. "Hey, if this guy is as good as you say he is, you should probably try to hold on to him."

Exactly.

CHAPTER SEVEN

Samantha glanced at William on the swing beside her. She pulled back on the chains and kicked her feet to scoop up air as the swing under her gained momentum.

He smiled. "This is fun. It's been forever since I've been on a playground."

"My brother, sister, and I used to come here all the time as children. We'd walk downtown and sometimes get ice cream."

"Kingsburg seems like a great town."

Samantha knew her face beamed with hometown pride, but she couldn't help it. She loved this little town. "I think so."

He pointed to the water tower. "I love the teapot."

"It's cute, isn't it? That and the dala horses

around town boast of the town's Swedish heritage."

"I thought I saw a lady dressed up in a Swedish outfit this morning going into one of the shops."

She smiled. "Yes, you did! Wait until we have the Swedish Festival in May. It's a lot of fun."

"May. Will you be back in time for that?"

She frowned. "I'll have to check when finals are."

"I'm going to miss you like crazy."

Her heart skipped a beat at his pronouncement. Did he truly care for her? "Do you mean that?"

"I wouldn't have said it if I didn't."

"I'll miss you too." She'd entertained the thought of transferring to Reedley College to finish up her degree, but she wasn't sure if she was ready to be this close to Jaime and Travis. Not yet.

"We'll both be busy, so hopefully it'll go by fast."

"Yeah." She smiled.

He hopped off the swing.

"What are you doing?"

He held out his hand to help her off. "Come on. Let's go get one of those ice creams you were talking about."

"But it's cold."

"The best time for ice cream. Seriously, though. Is there really a bad time for ice cream?"

She laughed. "You have a point."

He reached for her hand as they walked through the nearly deserted streets. "Something's been bothering you. Want to talk about it?"

How could he read her like that? She hadn't said anything at all, yet he could sense something amiss. Amazing.

She shrugged. "My sister and I are at odds right now."

He nodded.

"She's engaged to a guy I used to date."

"I see." He frowned and his eyes briefly flashed some undefinable emotion. "So, you still have feelings for this guy?" *Insecurity, perhaps?*

"No. I mean, I did, for a long time. But not anymore." *Not since you.*

"So, what's the problem?"

"I guess I'm just upset because I feel like she betrayed me. I come home from college and there's my ex-boyfriend sitting at my parents' table, with my sister wearing his engagement ring." She shook her head. "And expecting his baby."

"Oh, man. I think I can see why you'd be miffed about something like that."

"I'm sorry. I probably shouldn't have mentioned

that last part. My parents don't even know yet."

He zipped his lips. "Your secret's safe with me. But at least I'll know what to pray about."

"I appreciate that. Why is it I feel like I can tell you anything?"

William smiled. "Comes with the job description, I think."

"Perhaps."

"You know what I suggest you do?"

"No, what?"

"Forgive her. Forgive your sister and your ex and move on with your life. There's nothing good that can come out of resentment or bitterness."

"But how? How can I just forget about everything they've done and move on?"

"The Bible said that if we commit our works to the Lord, then our thoughts will be established. We must step out in faith *first*. Then God will illuminate the path before us."

"It's hard."

He nodded and gently squeezed her hand. "It is. But it's not impossible. Especially now that you have God in your life. Samantha, God will be with you in whatever you do. You are His child now."

"What do I need to do?"

William shrugged. "Go to your sister. Tell her about your feelings. Talk it out. And tell her that you've forgiven her."

"But I don't feel like I *have* forgiven her. I mean, I want to but..." She shrugged. "I don't know."

"You have it wrong, sweetheart. You're thinking that forgiveness is a feeling. It's not. It's a willful act. It's taking the burden you're carrying and offering it to God to carry for you. He wants to do that for you, but you have to let Him. Just give it to God, Samantha."

"Okay."

"Come here." He pulled her into his arms and she felt the press of his lips against her hair. "I'm proud of you. You can do this."

And in that moment, in William's embrace and God's strength, she knew she could.

CHAPTER EIGHT

"You're back early," Mom kissed Samantha's cheek as soon as she divested herself of her winter coat and hung it on the hall tree.

"Yeah. Pastor Marshall had plans for William to meet some of the church people tonight." She took a whiff of the air. "Dinner smells good."

"I made your favorite – roasted chicken and mashed potatoes." Mom beamed.

Samantha leaned over and kissed her mother's cheek. "Thanks, Mom. You're the best."

"I know," she teased. "Go wash up. It should be ready in about ten minutes."

"Okay." Samantha exited the foyer and noticed Jaime had been sitting on the couch, reading a book. She stopped and looked at her sister. "Can we talk?"

"Yeah, sure. Where?"

Samantha's gaze roamed the empty room. "Here is fine." She joined her sister on the sofa.

"Okay." Jaime looked away.

How did one go about a conversation like this, anyway? "You know I've been seeing William."

Jaime nodded.

"What do you think of him?"

"You're asking my opinion? Why would you want it?"

"Just curious."

"He seems nice. But then again, most guys do at first."

Indignation rose in Samantha's throat. "What do you mean *at first*? Has Travis done something to you?"

"No, nothing like that. He's just," she sighed, "distant, I guess." She absently rubbed her abdomen and regret filled Samantha's heart.

"Have you told Mom and Dad?" She whispered.

"No. I can't get the nerve to. Travis is coming over after you leave and we decided we're going to tell them together."

"Listen, Jaime. I just wanted to let you know that I forgive you. Truly."

Tears rushed to her sister's eyes and spilled onto

her cheeks. "Thank you. You don't know how much that means to me."

"When do you plan to get married?"

Jaime blew out a breath and shrugged. "I'm thinking after we tell Mom and Dad and Travis' parents, they'll want us to marry right away. We'll probably just go to the courthouse or something." She laughed bitterly. "Not exactly the fairy tale wedding I'd always dreamt about."

"So, you'll be married when I come back from college." Samantha gave a silent prayer of thanks that *she* wasn't the one in her sister's predicament. She easily could have been. "Do you love him?"

"Yes, I do."

"Then that's what matters, right?"

Jaime shrugged. "I'm not sure how he feels about me. I mean, he'd once said that he loved me but...I don't know, maybe he's just scared."

What was that verse William had shared earlier? "Sometimes you have to step out on faith and then the rest will come along." She knew she'd butchered it, but it went something like that, didn't it?

"I can tell you've been spending time with a preacher." Jaime smiled.

"Did that make any sense? What I just said?"

"I think so."

Their mother peeked her head around the corner. "Dinner's ready, girls." She disappeared just as quickly.

"Okay," the chorused.

Samantha took Jaime's hand. "I really want to talk to you about something before I leave for school, okay?"

"Is it about God?" Worry knitted her brow.

"How did you know?"

"I can just tell. Listen, Samantha. You don't have to tell me I'm a sinner. I'm well aware of that fact."

"God doesn't want to offer you condemnation, he wants to offer you hope." She stood up at their mother's call. "We'll talk more about it tonight, okay?"

At Jaime's nod, Samantha breathed a silent prayer for wisdom. Surely God was working things out in their lives. Somehow, Samantha could sense it was so. But more than anything, she was thankful that He'd restored their relationship.

William had been right. She'd just needed to step out in faith.

William set Samantha's carryon suitcase down and pulled her close. He clang to her with a fierceness she'd never known. "Oh, man. This is hard. I don't want to let you go." She not only heard, but felt the emotion in his voice.

She echoed his sentiments. "I don't have to go. I could transfer to Reedley."

He pulled back and gazed into her eyes. "But then you might lose credits, right? I don't want you to do that. And, you spent money on a plane ticket. It would be a waste." He brushed her cheek with his thumb. "Besides, they say absence makes the heart grow fonder. I guess we'll be testing out that theory."

"I want a kiss before I go." She noticed conflicting emotions in his eyes, he clearly wanted to kiss her as much as she wanted him to. "Just one?" she pleaded.

His mouth lowered to hers and offered the most achingly beautiful kiss she'd ever known. Several seconds passed before he finally forced himself away, but fire still burned in his eyes. He groaned. "I miss you already." Perhaps going away *would* be a good thing – for *both* of them.

A call over the intercom told her that if she didn't leave soon, she wouldn't make it at all. Fortunately, the line for security was short and she'd be able to zip through.

He released her from his embrace. "You'd better go. I love you."

"You do?"

"Yes. Now, go before you miss your flight." William carried her suitcase as far as he could and stood watching as she jumped through all the security hoops.

"Don't forget to write me," she called out above the other passengers in line.

"I won't."

Samantha waved and blew him a kiss before she turned and entered the corridor, then took off in a sprint toward the gate.

"I love you too, William," she whispered as she now sat on the plane and readied for takeoff. She stared out the window until they were well in the air and imagined William driving in one of the vehicles that were now too microscopic to identify.

This was going to be the longest semester of her life.

CHAPTER NINE

Samantha grinned when Tammy danced into their apartment, holding up an envelope.

"Hmm...I wonder who this might be from," Tammy teased.

Samantha quickly snatched the letter from her friend's hand and rushed to her tiny bedroom to devour its contents. She'd only been back at school for a month, but it seemed like an eternity. This was the second letter she'd received from William since Christmas break.

Dear Samantha,

I hope this letter finds you well. I miss you a lot.

The ministry is going well and our youth group has grown by one member. That may not seem like much to us, but to God, one person is a big deal. Please pray that I can minister to these kids as God leads.

How's school going? I hope you're doing your best so you can come back home as soon as possible. I'd be counting the days until you return, but that's too depressing. Instead, I'll keep myself busy and try not to think about how much I miss you.

I realized yesterday that I don't have a picture of you. Will you send me one? I think seeing a photo of your lovely face every day will help me to remember the great time we had over Christmas vacation, and lessen the burden of your absence.

I'd love to come see you, but I can't afford it right now. The ministry is more a labor of love than anything. In other words, being a youth pastor at a small church doesn't pay much. But I'm happy knowing that I'm where God wants me to be.

I'll be waiting for your next letter.

Love in Christ,

William

Samantha reread the letter then clutched it to her chest. William was right. Being away from each other was much more difficult than she thought it would be. They'd ultimately agreed to a long-distance courtship, in spite of the risks.

Finding William had been a dream come true. She'd once thought that about Travis, but now she saw the stark contrast between the two men. William constantly put others' needs above his own, whereas Travis had only exhibited selfishness.

Just knowing William made her want to strive to be a better person. He exemplified kindness and compassion. In their short time together before coming back to school, he'd inquired about where the homeless shelters were. He'd said he wanted to go and serve in their soup kitchen. Samantha hadn't even known what a soup kitchen was, let alone ever served in one.

She didn't doubt William would find plenty of good deeds to occupy himself while she was gone. She'd definitely found a keeper.

William continued to write faithfully every other week, like clockwork. Samantha enjoyed their letter courtship immensely, although she would much rather see him in person. Her birthday came and went and she found that she missed him more each day. He'd sent her a large beautiful bouquet of flowers and a note.

Happy Birthday, to the girl of my dreams.
Love, William

The only way life could get any better is if she were home and she could see William regularly. Samantha had all but forgotten about Travis. In only a month and a half, she'd complete her studies and be on her way home for good. The days couldn't pass soon enough.

It had been three weeks since Samantha's birthday. William hadn't sent any correspondence since the note with her flowers that day. She'd written to him twice now, but received no answer. At first, she figured he'd gotten busy and couldn't find extra time. But now, she was beginning to worry.

She called the church yesterday and asked for him. When they put her through to his private number, he didn't answer. *What could be wrong?* It wasn't like William to just stop communicating. Was this his way of breaking up with her? She'd thought the way Travis had broken up was bad, but at least *he'd* sent a text message.

After speaking with the church secretary to make sure William was okay, Samantha left a message for him to call her. She waited several days, but the return call never came. She'd thought about sending her sister to enquire of him, but thought better of it after remembering what had happened with Travis. Although she'd since made amends with Jamie, at William's prompting, she wasn't about to grant her sister her full-fledged trust.

When Samantha's friends suggested that maybe he'd found someone else, she'd broken down in tears. They confirmed her own dreadful suspicions. She came to the painful realization that their relationship was most likely over.

William had been right all along. Long-distance relationships didn't stand a chance of survival. Why hadn't she listened to him in the first place? Was that why he discouraged their relationship at the start? Because he wasn't truly interested? Or had he discovered the truth of her past and found someone else, with purity standards that matched his? She'd wanted to tell him about her past and about Travis, but she didn't want him to think less of her.

All this time, she'd been a fool. Physical pain gripped her heart. It felt as though her heart had been trampled under the hooves of a Belgian horse. She allowed the tears to flow freely. She'd been fooled by love twice now, and she was determined to never let it happen again. It wasn't worth the pain it caused.

She forced her tears away as frustration took over. She was *so sure* that William would be different, but it turns out he was just like all the other guys in the world. Wasn't a pastor supposed to be different – a cut above? Wasn't he supposed to set an example for others to follow? Well, a fine example he was setting – telling a girl that he loved her, then just disappearing off the face of the earth.

Were *all* men the same? Apparently so.

CHAPTER TEN

Samantha didn't care if she made a fool out of herself. She wanted answers.

"I'd like to see William, please." She stood in front of the receptionist's desk at the church office.

"I'll see if he's available." The receptionist rose from her cushioned office chair and walked down a short hall. She knocked on one of several doors that lined the hallway.

Samantha strained to hear the conversation, to no advantage.

The receptionist returned. "I'm sorry. He's unavailable right now."

"Is someone else in the office with him?" She tapped her foot impatiently.

"No, but–"

That's all she needed to hear. Samantha marched

down the hall to William's office. She heard the receptionist protesting, but ignored her.

She pushed the door open and burst into William's office. "I want to know why you stopped writing to me. Why didn't you answer any of my letters?" she demanded. Her arms crossed firmly over her chest.

William rose from his chair and closed the door behind her. "I thought that would be obvious. You're not the girl I thought you to be."

He must've discovered her past relationship with Travis. What else could it be? Had William run into Travis while she was gone? She'd feared that he'd react this way when he discovered the truth.

"I'm sorry. I can't change the past." She frowned. "Listen, William. I know I should have been honest with you up front. I just thought that if you knew that Travis and I slept together, you'd react this way."

"You *slept* with him *too*?!" He dug both hands into his hair and he shook his head. This was the first time she'd seen William upset.

"What do you mean, 'too'? Isn't that what we're discussing?"

"I should have listened to my conscience. It was a

mistake to ever agree to a long-distance relationship. I knew it would never work. We'd only been apart a few months and you're not only dating, but have also been intimate with another guy. Samantha, I thought I could trust you. I wrote you. I told you that I loved you. I guess all that wasn't enough."

"What are you talking about? What happened with Travis and I was two years ago."

"Two years ago?" William scratched his head and frowned. "I'm confused."

"Not as confused as I am."

He thrust his hands into his pockets. "Who's Travis?"

"Travis was my ex-boyfriend who's now married to my sister."

"And he came to your college?"

"What? You're totally confusing me. No. I *only* dated Travis in high school. He broke up with me and that's *why* I went off to college."

"I don't know what's going on."

"All I know is *you* stopped writing to me and I wanted to find out why. I thought maybe you'd started seeing some else." Her lip began quivering.

"Seeing someone el–?" His brow lowered. "No! *I* have not been the one seeing someone else."

"What's that supposed to mean? Are you implying that *I* have?"

"No, I'm not *implying* anything. I'm stating a simple fact."

"I don't know what you mean."

"Why won't you admit it, Samantha? I already know the truth. Don't lie about it; I hate lying. Just admit that you've been seeing someone else!" His hands clenched tightly at his sides.

She stared at him blankly.

"Let me refresh your memory. A bar. A dance. A kiss. Your birthday."

"Tammy and Jill took me out to the grill for my birth–" Samantha's eyes bulged. "You think that I was seeing Jace Armstrong?" She shook her head. "I'm not, nor have I *ever* been interested in Jace. Yes, I danced with him – out of kindness and nothing else. Yes, he kissed me – without permission. It earned him a good kick in the shin." She stared at William. "Wait a minute. How do *you* know about that? Who told you?"

"I saw it with my own two eyes."

"But how?"

"I wanted to surprise you on your birthday. As it turned out, the surprise was on me." He grimaced.

"You were there? You came to see me on my birthday?" *William came to the college?* It would have been so wonderful to have seen him.

He nodded. "I took a second job so I could earn extra money. I had this great evening planned for us." The hurt in William's eyes pulled on her heartstrings more than she cared to admit.

"I got the flowers, but..." Now it all made sense. *No wonder he never wrote back to me.* How would she have felt if she'd been in the same situation? Absolutely rotten. "I-I don't know what to say, William. Here, I thought that *you* were seeing someone else...and you thought..." She frowned. "I'm sorry."

"Yeah. Me too. I was furious when I left. I said some things that needed to be repented of," he admitted. "I even took some time off work." He sighed.

"Can we just do this over? Please?"

"I don't want to do it over. The first time around was awful enough."

"I meant *differently* this time."

"I know. I was teasing." The sadness in his eyes vanished. "Listen, Samantha. About Travis...I never expected you to be perfect. We all make mistakes we have to live with."

"You forgive me?"

"Of course. I just wish…" He walked around to the other side of his desk and opened the top drawer. He handed her a small wrapped gift. "This was supposed to be your birthday present."

She stared at him in astonishment.

"Please, open it."

She looked down at the gift he held out, and then received it from his hand. It had to be jewelry of some kind, she guessed, due to the size of the box; however, the box was the wrong size and shape for a ring. She carefully tore off the wrapping paper and lifted the small lid. Between two cushioned pads, a beautiful single diamond ring sparkled.

Her breath caught and she studied William's gaze. What could this mean? "William, I…"

"I hope it fits. I didn't really know what size." He shrugged.

Her eyes begged the question.

"I was going to ask…I mean, if you wanted to…" He raked a hand through his hair. "Sheesh, I'm so clumsy at this, it's not even funny."

She smiled and waited patiently for William to find the words he was searching for. The words she was hoping for.

"I was hoping we could be married by next Christmas. *This* Christmas, I mean. I'd like to take you home to meet my folks."

"Yes." She bit her bottom lip. He was every bit as sweet as she'd previously thought.

"Yes?"

She couldn't help the tears that formed in her eyes. "Yes, William. I'll marry you."

"Is December too soon for you? It will have been a year since we first met. I was thinking the twenty-third."

"December's perfect." Samantha smiled.

EPILOGUE

William's parents retired to bed nearly an hour ago. He and Samantha now snuggled on the love seat and sipped hot cocoa.

"I want to show you something." William reached for Samantha's hand and gently pulled her from the couch. They walked hand-in-hand to the brightly-lit Christmas tree. "See this ornament?"

Samantha smiled at the lovely glass ornament that contained a replica of an old ship. The lights from the tree flashed, illuminating their faces every few seconds. "It's beautiful."

"I bought this for you – for us, actually." He removed the ornament from the branch and placed it in her free hand. "This ship represents our love. Like a ship on the sea, we'll most likely weather some difficult storms. The glass globe represents

God. As long as the two of us stay under the protection of God's love, we'll be able to weather *any* storm that comes."

"What if the glass breaks?"

He took the ornament from her hand and dropped it on the floor.

Samantha's eyes widened when it hit the floor. "Amazing. It didn't break!"

William smiled. "Neither will God's love."

Samantha picked up the ornament and placed it back on the tree. "You're all a woman could ever dream for in a husband." She caressed his clean-shaven face and stepped on her tip-toes to plant a kiss on his cheek.

William left Samantha's side and went to an old-fashioned phonograph his parents kept on the corner table. He pulled out a record and carefully placed the player's needle on the outside threads.

When the music began, William held out his hand. "May I have this dance, my sweet wife?"

Samantha happily set her mug of cocoa down and joined her husband of two days. As the music played to 'Let it Snow', Samantha recalled all that God had done and how good He'd been to her.

She briefly broke away from William's intimate

embrace. "This is the second best Christmas I've ever had."

He bent down and pressed his lips to hers once again. William gazed into her eyes. "When was your first best Christmas?"

Samantha beamed. "Last year. When I met the two greatest men who've ever lived – you and Jesus."

THE END

Thank you for reading!

If you enjoyed this book, you'll want to sign up for Michelynn Christy's newsletter. By doing so, you'll be able to download a FREE ebook.
Click here: blessedpublishing1@gmail.com

Other titles by **Michelynn**:
Love Unawares
If He Only Knew
A Bride for Christmas

Other holiday titles available from
Blessed Publishing:

A Christmas of Mercy by J.E.B. Spredemann
Christmas in Paradise by J.E.B. Spredemann

A

Bride

FOR
CHRISTMAS

Michelynn Christy

Published by Blessed Publishing
Cover design by *iCreate Designs*
Formatting by Polgarus Studio

CHAPTER ONE

I sure am going to miss this place.

William Harper pulled the last few items from his desk and sighed. He glanced around his bedroom, the one he'd occupied his entire life minus the few years he'd spent in Bible college, the walls now barren of the inspirational quotes that oftentimes spurred him to greater heights.

Like now, he mused.

Leaving home was bittersweet indeed. He knew God had called him to California and exciting new adventures awaited him. That wasn't what unsettled him. It was moving at this time of the year. Leaving just before Christmas wasn't something he'd been planning on. This was, in fact, the first Christmas he'd be spending apart from his family. Even while in college, he'd returned home for Christmas.

The original plan had been to drive out to California in the spring. And that was how things would have played out had he not received the emergency phone call yesterday. Pastor Marshall apparently had some sort of accident. The poor elderly gentleman had stepped into a gopher hole, he'd sheepishly explained to William over the phone, and inadvertently sprained his ankle. William couldn't imagine having his entire leg in a cast. He couldn't fathom being in his seventies with that same predicament. So, naturally, he had agreed to start his new job as youth pastor, and helper to Hope Baptist Church's senior pastor, a few months early.

He could only trust that God had a plan for this situation, as He always did. But what on earth could it be?

"We sure will miss you, son," William's father engulfed him in a bear hug.

"I'll miss you and Mom too, Dad." He embraced his mother as well and glanced around the living room. He sure would miss this place.

"You'll call us and let us know you arrived safely?"

"Yes, Mom. Thanks for inviting everyone over to share an early Christmas supper with me." William eyed his father out of his peripheral vision, slipping out the front door.

"I'm just sorry your grandma couldn't make it." His mother sighed.

William frowned. "I don't know if she would have remembered anyway. You know how quickly her mind is slipping away."

"I wish it wasn't so. But at least you got to visit with her last week."

"Okay, Mom, I better get going now or I might just miss my flight. I think Dad's already waiting in the car." He lifted his suitcase and pecked his mother on the cheek one last time. "See ya later."

"Hopefully not too much later, Lord willing."

He noticed a slight misting of his mother's eyes as he stepped out the door.

William glanced down at his watch. *Three hours till my next flight.* He decided to find his departure terminal, then grab a bite to eat at one of the airport food kiosks nearby. After choosing a few items, he stepped in line. He placed his chicken wrap, sweet tea, and chips on the counter, careful to keep his carry-on close by lest it grow legs and walk away.

"That'll be seventeen dollars and fifty-two cents, please."

Seventeen dollars? He grudgingly pulled out a twenty and handed it to the cashier, who handed back his change. A mere two dollars and a few coins. He stared at it and grimaced.

Putting himself through college had been a hard lesson in frugality. Not that he'd paid for all of it, his parents had footed half the bill. He worked part-time for the remainder while keeping up with a full school schedule. It was not something he wished to repeat. He was so busy, he couldn't have gotten into trouble even if he wanted to.

He sat at an empty table and quickly bowed his head to give thanks for his food. When he opened his chicken wrap and nearly got it to his lips, his phone vibrated. He fished it from his pocket and glanced down at it to see who the caller was.

Marcus. He grinned.

Marcus had been his roommate and best buddy in Bible college. He hadn't seen him since they graduated in June, but they'd kept in touch over the past few months.

"Hey, Marc, what's up?"

"I was wondering if you'd like to get together

with some of the guys for New Year's Eve. We're going to hang out, enjoy some food and games, light some fireworks, you know. What do you say?"

"Ah, man. I wish I could." He watched as passengers headed to their terminals. "I'm actually on my way to California."

"California? Now? I thought you weren't going till this spring?"

"Change of plans. They need me now."

"So, where are you?"

"Sitting in an airport in Dallas. I have a three hour layover."

"Bummer. Hey, I hear there are lots of pretty girls in California."

William laughed. "There are a lot of pretty girls everywhere."

"Yeah, I guess you're right about that." Marcus chuckled. "Hey, speaking of pretty girls, I got a text from Jessica yesterday." His tone sobered.

"And?"

"She wanted my address so she could send my promise ring back. I guess she met some guy and they're getting pretty serious."

"I'm sorry to hear that, man." William frowned.

"It is what it is. I thought she might have been the

one, but I guess God has other plans."

"That's a positive way to look at it."

"It hurts to look at it any other way."

"I can imagine."

"Well, look, I'll let you go now. We'll miss you at the New Year's party."

"Tell the guys hello for me, will ya?"

"Will do. You take care and keep in touch. And don't let some pretty girl steal your heart."

William chuckled. "I doubt that'll happen."

"Hey, you never know."

"Bye, Marcus." He clicked off the phone after his friend returned his farewell.

He thought about Marcus' words. It seemed like a romantic relationship was a long way off for him. In fact, he'd never had a serious relationship with any girl—hadn't even kissed one. Just the thought warmed his insides.

It wasn't that girls didn't find him attractive or vice versa. For one, he was somewhat of an introvert so he didn't go out of his way to meet those of the female kind. Second, he figured that if God had a girl for him, then *He* would bring her to him. God didn't need his help. God knew when he would be ready and His timing was perfect.

CHAPTER TWO

William settled into the window seat, thankful for the extra leg room in this flight compared to his last one. Fortunately, there was an empty seat between himself and the next passenger and he could breathe easier. He loathed being crammed in with strangers.

He covertly eyed the attractive young woman who shared his row. Headphones were strapped over her ears, her eyes closed. He wondered if she was listening to music or an audiobook. He wondered where she was going and what her life was like. He wondered if she had a significant other, which caused him to inadvertently glance down at her hand.

Whoa! Where on earth did that *thought come from? Marcus.*

He reprimanded himself, then hastily searched

his carry-on bag for a much needed distraction. He pulled out his Bible. Yes, he should be reading his Bible. Not dwelling on the marital status of a beautiful young woman he'd never met.

William sighed and looked out the window to try and regather his thoughts. He haphazardly opened his Bible and chanced a glance inside. *Let him kiss me with the kisses of his mouth...*

He slammed the Bible shut. *The Song of Solomon*?

He forced his eyes closed. *Lord, what on earth are You trying to show me? Help me with my thoughts, Lord. I want to serve You. I want my thoughts to be pleasing to You.*

William's eyes popped open. He must've fallen asleep. He looked at his watch. Just forty-five minutes until he was scheduled to arrive. Good. The sooner he got out of this seat, the better.

His gaze moved to the middle-aged flight attendant walking past their row, then landed on the passenger next to the empty seat between them.

Was she crying? He frowned.

Yep. The swiping away of a tear was unmistakable.

What should I do, Lord? Should I do anything? Should I say something to her? He would have opened his Bible for inspiration but he wasn't taking any chances after the last time he tried that.

He fiddled with his hands, then reached for the airline catalog in the back pocket of the seat front of him. Surely, this would provide a distraction. He turned the page and something caught his eye. He laughed out loud, causing the young woman next to him to look his way.

"Oh, I'm sorry if I bothered you." He frowned.

She smiled. *She smiled. I got her to smile!*

Apparently, that had been the boost of confidence he needed to continue the conversation. William showed her the funny ad in the catalog. They spoke casually for a few moments, as though they were old friends. He discovered that her name was Samantha. *A lovely name for a lovely girl.*

"Where are you headed to?"

"Fresno." She grinned.

"Me, too." *Idiot! Of course, you're both going to Fresno.* It wasn't like the plane had any other destination. "Well, not exactly. I'll be getting a ride to Kingsburg. Do you know where it is?"

Another smile. "That's actually where I'm going too. I was pretty much born and raised there." The wheels rumbled as the plane touched down.

Of all the chances... *Lord?*

"I told my mom I'd call her as soon as we arrived. She's supposed to come pick me up." She pulled out her cell phone and swiped the screen, probably taking the setting off Airplane Mode.

The passengers around them began to gather their things from the overhead compartments and deplane.

"There's no need to do that. I mean, I'm already going there. You're welcome to ride along. I'm sure that Brother Anderson won't mind. He's the deacon that's supposed to pick me up." He removed his carry-on from under the seat in front of him, then stood. "Do you have anything in the overhead compartment?"

She moved into the aisle. "Yeah, one suitcase."

He opened the lid and spied an unmistakably feminine pink and purple plaid suitcase with wheels. "This it?"

She nodded and he brought it down for her. "Thanks."

"My pleasure. Do you have any checked baggage?" He gestured for her to precede him as they began their journey toward the airplane's exit.

"Nope. This is it. Just the one carry-on." They

walked side by side until they were in the main part of the airport. "Mr. Anderson, you said?"

He nodded.

"Is his name Clive?" Her face brightened.

He rubbed his chin. "I believe so." He quirked a brow. "You know him?"

"His daughter and I were good friends at Rafer Johnson." She must've noticed his puzzled looked and continued. "It's the junior high school, named after a local Olympian."

"Interesting."

"Anyway, my friend Jennifer Anderson died in a car accident when we were in high school." She frowned.

"Oh, man. That's terrible."

"Yeah. The person driving was under the influence. He died too. It was a tragedy for the whole community."

"I bet." *Lord, this community really does need You. Help me to shine Your light here. Use me as You wish.*

CHAPTER THREE

William glanced around the spare bedroom provided by Pastor Marshall. Homesickness had already begun creeping in. It had commenced the moment he'd arrived at the pastor's house. The rose bushes had been the culprit. They reminded him of Mom. She'd always loved roses.

He stretched out on the full size bed, his feet slightly dangling off. He'd been looking forward to relaxing a little bit before tomorrow night's candlelight service.

He closed his eyes and immediately thought of the pretty young woman that had captured his attention. She'd said she didn't go to church anywhere. Did that mean she wasn't saved? *Not necessarily.* If only they'd had more time to talk. At least he now knew where she was staying. Not that he would just stop by her parents' place and say hello.

No. If God wanted them to reconnect, He would orchestrate a meeting like He had on the plane. Or had that just been a coincidence? The thought of never seeing Samantha again bothered him more than he cared to admit.

"William?" A muffled voice called through the door.

He hopped up from the bed and pulled the door open. "Pastor Marshall?"

"Uh, yes. Sorry to bother you, son." He frowned. "I'm wondering if you can do me a favor?"

"Sure. What is it?"

"The jewelry store at the mall just called. I ordered something special for my wife for Christmas." He whispered and glanced down the hall. "Would you mind picking it up for me? You may take my car."

"No problem. Just give me the address and I can punch it in to the GPS on my phone. How far is it?"

"About forty-five minutes or so, depending on how fast you drive and how heavy traffic is." He reached into his pocket. "Here are the keys. I've already paid for the gift, so you'll just need to give him my name. You may call me if you have any problems."

"Okay. I'll probably grab a bite to eat while I'm out, so please let your wife know I won't be eating supper here."

"Take as long as you'd like, William. Thank you. I really appreciate this."

"I don't mind at all, Pastor Marshall."

William took the bag from the jeweler's hand and turned to leave the store. *No way!*

"Samantha?"

She turned from the case she'd been perusing and eyed the package in his hand. "William, right?"

"That's me." Apparently, she hadn't been thinking as much about him as he had of her. He didn't think he'd ever forget her name. Noticing the question in her eyes, he glanced down at the package he was holding. "Oh, yeah. Pastor Marshall asked me to get something for him since he's out of commission."

She nodded and smiled. "I'm getting something for my sister."

"That's nice." He noted the several packages in

her hand. "Do you have more shopping to do?"

"No, this is my last purchase."

"I was about to go grab a bite to eat. Would you like to join me?"

Surprise marked her features. "Oh. Uh, sure. What do you have in mind?"

"Do you like fish?"

"I love it. You?"

He nodded.

"There's a pretty good little seafood place across the street. Would you like to go there?"

"I think I might have seen that. Sounds great." He smiled.

Okay, God. This has to *be from You!*

William listened as the beautiful girl across the table spoke. He'd asked her about the city and she'd quickly filled him in on Fresno and the surrounding areas.

"You're going to die here in the summer. It's so hot!"

He frowned. "Really?"

"My advice? Find someone with a pool. Does your pastor have one?"

"I don't think so."

"We don't either. It's something I always wanted growing up, but we never did get one. At least we aren't that far from the beach."

"How far is it?"

"About two and half hours to Morro Bay."

"That doesn't sound too bad."

"No, it's not. Not really. My friends and I went every summer in high school."

He did his best to try to *not* picture Samantha in a bathing suit. He needed to redirect his thoughts. Fast. "How's your clam chowder?"

"It's great. Do you like your fish and chips?"

"Yep. Hey, thanks for coming to eat with me. It's much more fun than eating alone."

She nodded. "Thanks for asking."

"Are you free tomorrow night? I'd like to invite you to the Christmas Eve service at the church. Does that sound like something you'd be interested in?"

"I'm not really a church person. Sorry." She shrugged. "I've never really been keen on the whole church thing."

William felt like he was inside a large balloon and somebody had just taken a needle and popped it. To him, church was practically his life. He couldn't imagine living apart from it. He did his best to hide his disappointment. "Oh. Well, the invitation still stands, if you happen to change your mind."

"I appreciate that."

❧

William stared up at the ceiling hoping sleep would come, but no matter what he did, it eluded him. It was times like this he wondered if God meant for him to pray about something—or someone, perhaps? But right now, the only person that occupied his thoughts was Samantha.

He sat up. *Lord, why do I feel this special connection to her? Is there a reason our paths keep crossing?*

SHE NEEDS ME.

Of course! Why hadn't he seen it before? Samantha wasn't saved and God must be calling her. Apparently, God must want to use him to lead Samantha to Him. *Lord, if this is what You want me to do, please open a door.*

William yawned and his eyelids now felt heavy. That had to be it—the reason God wouldn't let him sleep. As soon as his head hit the pillow, dreamland became a reality.

CHAPTER FOUR

Contrary to popular belief, not all pastors minded wearing suits. At least, William didn't mind. He felt that the attire earned him a certain level of respect and enacted confidence in himself, which he didn't feel when dressed in casual attire.

He'd chosen non-traditional colors for the season—a black suit, blue shirt, and a tie that brought the colors together. Mom had always said these colors complemented him. Hopefully, Samantha would think the same. *You don't even know if she's coming tonight,* he chided himself.

But he'd been praying that she would. What better time to meet the Saviour than at Christmas? Although, he acknowledged that God's timing was perfect—not his own. He closed his eyes once again and prayed that God would soften Samantha's heart.

William scanned the doors again as the musicians began playing the background music. The congregants began taking their seats and the pews started filling up quickly.

He stood next to Pastor Marshall as the older man explained how the service would play out. "I will introduce you to the congregation at the beginning of the service, then you'll be free to take a seat."

William nodded and hoped he wouldn't ask him to speak to the congregation. Just then, he glanced again toward the entrance, hoping beyond hope that Samantha would walk through the doors. *Nope.*

He sighed and resigned himself to the fact that she probably wasn't coming. After all, she said she didn't do the church thing. If she only knew it wasn't some 'thing' one 'did.' He'd wanted to explain that then and there, but he didn't want to sound pushy or turn her off. But maybe he should have. Perhaps that was the reason she hadn't shown up.

He glanced at the door again and smiled. *Or maybe not.*

"Excuse me, Pastor Marshall. There's someone here that I need to greet." His gaze met Samantha's and she smiled. His heart did a little flip-flop.

"Just don't be too long. We'll be starting soon."

"I'll be back as soon as I can."

He hurried down the stairs and met Samantha as she waded through the congregants who were still standing.

He grinned as he approached. She had no idea how happy he was to see her here tonight. "Hi! I'm glad you made it."

She looked down at her jeans and grimaced. "I hope I'm not underdressed."

"Oh, no. You look great." *Wonderful, actually.* Did she have any idea how mesmerizing her eyes were against the forest green sweater she wore?

"You look nice too. That's a great color for you."

Yep, Mom was right about the blue. "Let's grab a pew. I need to return to the stage but I should be back in just a little bit."

She nodded.

"You don't mind if I sit by you, do you?" He led the way to a row near the front.

"No, of course not. I don't see anyone else I know."

"Well, I guess we're in the same boat then because I don't know many people here either." He smiled and winked.

He looked toward the stage and noticed the leaders moving into their respective places. "I'd better go. I'll see you in a bit."

True to his word, he returned to Samantha's side after the pastor introduced him to the congregation. Just knowing he'd be sitting next to Samantha for the entire evening gave him an extra boost of confidence and excitement.

He nearly choked on his mint when the lady in the pew next to them asked if they were husband and wife. Hopefully, the woman's words wouldn't scare Samantha off.

"Just friends," he clarified. Was it his imagination or did Samantha's smile just dim a bit?

As the service continued, he glanced over at his visitor every now and then. She seemed to be enjoying the singing and listened intently as the assistant pastor preached.

He closed his eyes and gave thanks to God for everything He'd sacrificed to save mankind. The

Christmas hymns just heightened his appreciation for his Saviour—he never grew tired of singing about Jesus' birth and the wonderful miracle it was. What a gracious God he served.

He asked God to touch Samantha's heart as the preacher spoke. When he gave the altar call, Samantha raised her hand. William's heart leapt for joy and he nodded for her to follow him out to the foyer. This was the moment he'd been waiting for, hoping for, praying for. *Lord, please give me the words to say.*

He guided her to a couple of chairs in the corner. Just the two of them occupied the foyer at present and William was thankful. "You raised your hand." Did she catch his pleased tone?

"I did." She nodded, but concern darkened her features. "I'm not sure I'm on my way to Heaven. I mean, I've never really thought about that kind of thing before."

"And now?"

"Well, I think I've been a pretty decent person, you know. I'm not perfect, but I'd hope that God would let me into Heaven. I've never killed anyone or anything like that."

"So, you think that murderers should go to Hell?"

She shrugged. "I imagine so."

"Do you realize that God used murderers to write part of the Bible?"

Her mouth hung open. "No, I didn't."

"Yep. And adulterers, liars, all kinds of people who'd done wicked things."

"But isn't the Bible supposed to be God's book? I mean, I don't know much about it, but I thought it was supposed to be holy or something."

"You're absolutely right. And it is. See, God's standards are a lot different than ours. He takes our mistakes and turns them into something beautiful, like discarded scraps that are woven into a beautiful rug.

"And that is basically the message of the Bible. God saw the mess mankind had made and sent His Son Jesus to clean it up."

She frowned. "Are you talking about Jesus dying on the cross?"

"Exactly. Samantha, do you know why He did that?" He turned in his Bible to the book of John.

She shook her head. "Not exactly."

"The Bible says, '*For God so loved the world, that he gave his only begotten Son, that whosoever believeth in him should not perish, but have everlasting life. For God sent not his Son into the world to condemn the world; but that the world through him might be saved. He that believeth on him is not condemned: but he that believeth not is condemned already, because he hath not believed in the name of the only begotten Son of God.'* Do you understand?"

"I think so."

He handed her his Bible and pointed to the highlighted verses he'd just read. "So, going by these verses, what does one need to do to be saved?"

Her eyes scanned the verses. "To believe in God's Son?"

"Exactly!"

"It sounds...simple."

"Well, the Bible also states that '*God is not willing that any should perish, but that all should come to repentance.*' It's not His will for anyone to go to Hell. It was created for the devil and his angels. God made it so that even a small child could understand." He leaned forward in his chair. "Yet at the same time, God gives each of us a choice. He won't force His will on us–we can go to Hell if we want to."

"Who would want to?"

"There are plenty out there who are deceived by

the devil. They see God and His ways as restricting and confining, when in reality, it is the Truth that makes you free. The way to Heaven is narrow, and sadly, there are few who choose the narrow way."

"But you'd said that murderers wrote the Bible. I don't get that part."

"I believe that God has such a different view of mankind than how we think. His ways are not our ways, and His thoughts are not our thoughts.

"God is good. And in His goodness, He offers forgiveness, peace, and eternal life to *anyone* who places their faith solely in Him. It has absolutely nothing to do with our works, our good deeds. It's all about Him and His goodness, His love. We are His creation. He desires to have a relationship with each person, so they can know His goodness, so they can reflect His goodness and His love."

"Wow. That sounds amazing!"

"It is. God's grace is absolutely amazing!"

"I'd like to do that—to place my trust in Him— but I'm unsure how."

He admired the sincerity in her voice.

Thank you, Lord! "The Bible tells us to confess and believe. '*That if thou shalt confess with thy mouth the Lord Jesus, and shalt believe in thine heart that God hath raised him from the dead, thou shalt be saved.'* It's that simple. Would you like to pray now?"

"I'm not sure if I'll do it right."

"If it comes from your heart, it is right," he assured.

CHAPTER FIVE

"I enjoyed that service so much, thank you for inviting me." Samantha smiled and her beautiful hazel eyes met his.

"Me, too. We had candlelight services back home too, and they were always one of my favorite parts of the Christmas season." He took a sip of his hot drink. "Are you enjoying your cocoa?"

"Yes, it's yummy."

The night was going by way too fast for his taste. He needed to think of something so he could spend more time with Samantha. "Is there anything to do around here at this hour?"

She frowned. "Not too much. Oh, have you seen the dancing lights yet?"

"Dancing lights? Is that like a musical production or something?"

Samantha laughed. "No, silly. They're Christmas lights at a house out in the country."

"Just *one* house?"

She nodded. "Do you want to go? It'll be worth it, I promise."

He'd go even if there were no dancing lights. The truth was, he was smitten with this beautiful young lady. *Who is now a born again Christian*, he encouraged himself. Since that was now the case, what was holding him back from beginning a relationship with her?

He knew what it was. *She will soon go back to college.* That and his friend Marcus' experience with a love interest. It hadn't ended well for his friend. What made him think a relationship with Samantha would be any different?

"Was that a yes?"

He hushed his discouraging thoughts. "It's definitely a yes." His eyes met hers and he wondered if she could read his thoughts. He wanted to spend as much time with her as possible. Hopefully, she felt the same way.

"We can take my car," she offered.

"Sure. Um, let me just let Pastor Marshall know and make sure he doesn't need my assistance."

"Oh, wow! You were right. This is amazing." He watched intently as the colorful Christmas lights danced to the beat of the music.

"It's cool, isn't it?" He loved seeing her smile and the joy that radiated from her face. Had accepting Christ already made a difference in her life?

"You look happy."

"I am." She sighed. "I mean, not that everything in my life is peachy. But right now, being here with you..." Her voice trailed off and their eyes met.

William swallowed and understood the meaning behind Samantha's words. Without thinking things through, he leaned closer to her. It was almost like a magnet pulling them toward each other. When their lips met, his longing for her grew deeper. This feeling—whatever it was—was wonderful. His hands wrapped around her head and back and their kiss intensified. He was helpless to suppress the groan of pleasure that emerged from somewhere deep within.

A car pulled up beside them, and he immediately forced himself to break away. He chided himself for his carelessness.

"Is something wrong?"

Oh, no. Everything is right. Too right.

"I'm sorry, Samantha. I shouldn't have done that."

"Why not? Tell me you didn't enjoy it." She frowned.

"Oh, no, that's not the case at all." He grimaced. "I'm afraid I enjoyed it a little too much. Samantha, I'm the youth pastor. My life will be an open book in this community. I have to set a good example. An example of purity."

"I don't know if I understand."

"Samantha, I fully intend to save myself for marriage. In fact, that kiss we shared—it was my very first, my only one. I had wanted to save my first kiss for the woman I plan to marry." He rubbed his thumb over the top of her hand.

Her expression widened and her lips formed an 'O.' She didn't hide her surprise. "You'd never kissed—*anyone*?"

"Not until now. Just you."

"I'm...I don't know what to say...I'm honored that I was your first."

He didn't like the sound of that. *Your first.* As though she would be one in a long line of women who would receive his affection. That was the last thing he wanted. He wanted Samantha—and *only* Samantha. He didn't like the dating game and had no desire to be part of it. The human heart wasn't something to be toyed with. It was something to be cherished.

"You will leave for college soon."

She nodded. "I will."

What had he been thinking? He'd blown it, big time. Why did he kiss her? "I'm sorry."

"Sorry? For what?"

"I'd hoped to have a relationship with you, but I wasn't thinking. I will be here and you will be off at college. Long distance relationships hardly ever stay intact." He thought once again of Marcus. Here, his friend had been devoted and faithful, and in return he'd had his heart broken. That was the last thing he desired to go through, especially with a girl like Samantha.

"We can make it work."

Had Marcus' girlfriend said the same thing? "I wish that were true. But you'll be interested in other guys while you're in college. It's a long time to be apart."

"Have a little faith in me, William. You think I'll

run off with the first cute guy I see? I'm not as shallow as you must think I am."

"I'm sorry, I didn't mean for it to sound that way. It's just, I had a friend in college who attempted the same type of relationship and it didn't end well."

"That was them, not us. I really like you, William. I'd love to get to know you more."

He sighed, and a warning sounded off in his head. He quickly hushed the warning, choosing to hope for the best. "I'm willing to give it a try if you are."

"I want to do more than just try. I want this to work, William. Can we *make* it work?"

"I hope so. But I have one rule."

Her eyes sparkled. "What's your rule?"

"No kissing."

She frowned. "What? No kissing? But that's what people do when they're in lo...in a relationship."

"That kiss about did me in, Samantha. I will not be able to enter into marriage pure if we indulge ourselves, and I absolutely want to be pure for my wife."

Tears welled in her eyes and he didn't understand what he'd done wrong. Did she think she would not be the one? Did she *know* she would not be the one?

Perhaps he was a fool and was setting himself up for heartache. For failure.

"That's beautiful, William. I've never met anyone like you. You're truly wonderful."

Oh.

She turned the engine over and headed back in the direction of town. William watched as they passed various country houses decorated with lights. A cemetery, a school, and then a drive through downtown on Draper Street. Finally, they'd passed churches and a park, and before he knew it, they were outside of Pastor Marshall's home. Most of the drive back, they'd remained silent—most likely lost in their own thoughts. At least, that was William's case.

"I'm going to miss you when you're gone." He sighed at last.

She intertwined her fingers with his and he didn't want her to let go. "Well, until then, we'll spend as much time together as possible. Okay?"

"I'd like nothing better, but I'm sure I'll have some ministerial duties to complete. Is it okay if I call you tomorrow?"

"Yes, definitely. We usually have relatives over in the morning for breakfast and a gift exchange, but I should be free in the afternoon."

"I'll give you a call then. I'm still not sure what Pastor Marshall has planned for Christmas, so I can't make any commitments just yet, but I'd love to see you if I'm able."

She smiled and it tugged at his heart once again. He didn't even know what it was about Samantha—she was pretty and kind, but he couldn't place his finger on what exactly it was. Somehow, they'd just clicked.

He'd reasoned within himself that it could be God. After all, He had placed them on the same airline of the same flight to the same destination in the same row of the plane. Both of their trips had been impromptu, last minute flights. What were the odds?

He didn't know for certain, but he'd *almost* bet that Samantha was *the one* for him. And that thought thrilled him to the core.

CHAPTER SIX

William did his best to focus on the company that surrounded him–Pastor Marshall's teen grandchildren, who would most likely be in his youth class.

"All right, Pastor William, it's your turn," fourteen-year-old Isaiah encouraged.

He picked up one of the Pictionary cards and eyed the word. "Okay, this one is All Play. Who is drawing for your team?"

"It's my turn." Sixteen-year-old Jenna eyed him sheepishly. He had no doubt that the young lady had a crush on him.

"Okay, here you go." He slid the card to her facedown, and she purposely brushed his fingers.

She glanced at the card and her eyes lit with delight. "We've got this one, guys." She encouraged her teammates, challenging William at the same time.

William grinned. He admitted he was having a lot of fun, even though his thoughts often drifted to Samantha. "Oh, no. This one is all *ours*. Come on, guys, this one's easy. Watch my drawing."

One of the players flipped the timer and they began drawing feverishly.

"Lighthouse!" One of the other team members called out in record time.

William's mouth dropped open. "How did you get that so quickly?"

"You better close that or you're gonna catch flies. I thought you said you had that one, Pastor!" Jenna taunted and her teammates laughed.

"I hadn't even finished the base." He reached for her paper and examined her drawing. A scribbled lightbulb that was barely recognizable and a triangle on top of a square. *Lighthouse.*

"You have to think outside the box, Pastor William," one of the players suggested.

"And you have to be fast," Jenna said.

"All right, guys. Break time. I've gotta go make a phone call." He stood up from the game table.

"Who you calling?" One of them called out.

William grinned, but shook his head.

"I bet it's his girlfriend," Isaiah said.

"It is not," Jenna insisted. "He doesn't have a girlfriend."

"Is it, Pastor?" Isaiah asked.

Before leaving the room, William nodded and noticed Jenna's expression quickly sour. Better she find out now so she didn't try to pursue him. Hopefully, they'd spread the word so he didn't have a flock of young admirers following him around town.

Fortunately, she picked up on the second ring. "Hey, Samantha?"

"Yes, it's me. William?"

"How'd your family breakfast go?" He cupped the mouthpiece so she could hear him over the jovial outbursts going on in the other room.

"It went great. What are you doing?"

"I've been playing board games with Pastor Marshall's grandkids."

"Oh, that sounds like fun."

"It is, but I miss you." His tone softened.

"You do?"

"Definitely. Can I see you tonight?"

"Yeah, but where? I think everything's closed on Christmas day."

"How about we take a walk around your neighborhood?"

"We'd have to bundle up, but sure. That sounds great. What time?"

"Will seven work for you?"

"Seven sounds good. You can park in front of my house."

"I'd just planned on walking."

"Oh, okay. That works too. See you then." He could feel her smile through the phone. Hopefully, she was just as excited about this evening as he was.

"Pastor Marshall, the church wouldn't happen to have any extra gift and award Bibles, would they?"

Pastor Marshall smiled. "Are you in need of one?"

"Yes. A feminine Bible, preferably."

"I just so happen to have some extra gift and award Bibles in my office. Would you like to take a look to see if any of them will work?"

"I'd love to. Thanks, you're a real lifesaver."

"Nope, He is the Lifesaver." His host pointed to the ceiling and grinned as William pushed the pastor's wheel chair down the hall toward his office.

"Yes, He is indeed." He opened the door.

"Over there, on the top shelf of the bookcase is where I keep them. Take down as many as you'd like to look at."

William eyed the colorful Bible spines through the small plastic windows of the boxes and reached for a fuchsia one, remembering her pink and purple plaid carry-on suitcase. He brought it down and opened the box. He ran his hand over the soft leather cover. This would be perfect for Samantha.

"It's a King James?" William asked before he thought to look.

"That, it is. I love the old standby. That book has saved more souls than all the others combined. Did you know that?"

"No, I didn't." He turned to his pastor-friend and pulled out his wallet. "How much do I owe you?"

"Buy the truth and sell it not, the Good Book says. You owe me nothing, William. You have been a blessing to me and I'm happy to give it to you."

"Thank you very much, Pastor Marshall." He nodded and then grimaced, hating to ask another favor. "You wouldn't happen to have any wrapping paper, would you?"

"Now *that* would be my wife's department." He smiled.

CHAPTER SEVEN

William glanced down at the neatly wrapped package in his hand and hastened his step toward Samantha's house. Mrs. Marshall had been sweet to offer to wrap the gift for him, but he'd wanted to do it himself. It seemed a bit more personal that way. And so he did, but he took Mrs. Marshall's advice at each fold and closure. He did allow her to tie the expert bow for him, since he'd been clueless even after Mrs. Marshall's careful instructions.

He walked up the cement path that led to Samantha's current residence and knocked on the door, which opened almost immediately. He stared up at a tall young man, probably close to his own age.

"Is Samantha here?" His hands began to perspire just a bit.

The young man raised a brow. "You're the pastor, right?"

"Yes, sir. The youth pastor at Hope Baptist Church." He offered his hand. "My name's William."

He nodded and shook his hand. "Scott. Samantha's older brother."

"Nice to meet you, Scott." The guy was at least a few inches taller than him.

Samantha appeared behind her brother. "Scott, what are you doing? Aren't you even going to invite William in?"

Her brother stepped out of the way. "He's all yours, sis."

Samantha shook her head. "Please pardon my brother. Won't you come in? I can get us some cider for our walk."

William smiled and stepped inside. "Sure."

Within a couple of minutes, drinks in hand, they made their way into the fresh night air.

"I brought a little something for you." He handed her the gift.

"Oh, William, this is gorgeous! I hate to unwrap it, it's so pretty." Her hand caressed the bright paper. "You didn't wrap it yourself, did you?"

He nodded meekly and took the drink from her

hand so she could open the package.

"Are you serious?"

He shrugged. "Well, I admit I didn't tie the bow. Mrs. Marshall did that for me. Sheesh, you'd think it would be like tying your shoelaces. Not so. I definitely won't be taking up giftwrapping as a profession in the near future."

Samantha laughed. "Well, you did a fine job with the wrapping." She carefully slid her finger under the tape and gently opened one of the ends. "What is it?"

He shook his head, not willing to give away the surprise.

She slid the box out of the wrapping paper and read it. "It's a Bible."

"Do you have one yet?"

"No, I don't." She smiled and opened the box. Her hands caressed the soft leather. "This is awesome. It's so pretty. I didn't even know they made Bibles in pretty colors."

"Do you like it?"

"Yes, very much. I like to read. I've never owned one before."

"I'm sure you'll find it intriguing. Do you know much about it?"

"Not really. Just what we talked about last night."

"I'm excited for you. God's Word is amazing."

Her eyes sparkled under the moonlit sky. "Really?"

"Yep. It's basically God's story. If you start at Genesis, you'll discover how everything began. It's the beginning of time. And the last book is Revelation. It is the end of this world as we know it."

Her expression widened. "Wow, it does sound fascinating."

"But it's not exactly in chronological order. It's divided by subject matter."

"Subject matter?"

"Let me show you." He took the Bible and handed her drink back. They stopped under a street light and he set his own drink on the ground.

She picked it up. "I'll hold your cup."

He flipped the Bible open. "First of all, the Bible isn't one book but a collection of sixty-six books. Then, it's divided into two parts—the Old Testament and the New Testament." He showed her. "See?"

"Okay. So, it's sixty-six books?"

"Yes. Thirty-nine books in the Old Testament

and Twenty-seven books in the New Testament."

"Why are there two parts?"

"Good question. The Old Testament is looking forward to Christ's first coming. The New Testament begins just before the birth of Christ and then goes into the future."

"Wow, it sounds like a lot."

"It is. A person could read and study this book their whole life and not even scratch the surface of its depth."

"So, when I read it, should I start at the beginning?"

"I usually suggest two books to start with. John and Romans. The book of John is one of the Four Gospels—the Four Gospels are basically the life of Jesus Christ while he was on earth."

"Why are there four?"

William smiled. "They were written by four different men. Matthew, Mark, Luke, and John."

"Okay."

"So, while you'll read all about Jesus in John, Romans will help you discover who you are in Christ."

"Romans. Didn't you read me verses from there before?"

"Yes, Romans clearly lays out the plan of salvation—how one is saved."

"Okay."

He flipped the Bible open to the front section. "If you look in the front, you'll find a table of contents. That will help you figure out where the books are."

"Oh, there's writing inside!" She handed his drink back and took the Bible from him. "Dear Samantha, May you grow in grace and in the knowledge of Jesus Christ. With Love, William." She reached over and hugged him. "Oh, that's so sweet."

"I want you to call or text me if you have any questions when you're reading, okay?"

"Okay."

"May I share something with you?" He pointed to the book in her hands.

"Sure."

He took the Bible from her and opened it to the book of Acts. "I wanted to read you the story about Philip and the Ethiopian eunuch."

She listened intently, taking in each word of the story. "Wait. Stop. Read that verse again."

"Which one?"

"The one about the water and when the chariot stopped."

William chuckled. "Okay. I'll start at verse thirty-six. *And as they went on their way, they came to a certain water: and the eunuch said, See, here is water; what doth hinder me to be baptized? And Philip said, If thou believest with all thine heart, thou mayest. And he answered and said, I believe that Jesus Christ is the Son of God. And he commanded the chariot to stand still: and they went down both into the water, both Philip and the eunuch; and he baptized him.*"

"I thought that people usually got baptized when they were babies."

William frowned. "Yes, some religions practice that but you won't find that in the Bible."

"Really?"

"Yes. Everyone we read about who was baptized in the Bible, like the Ethiopian eunuch, was a professed believer in Jesus Christ. And here Philip tells him what is required for baptism—to believe with all your heart."

"But how can babies believe? They don't know or understand yet."

William shrugged, not really wanting to start a

debate. "I'm not sure, because I wasn't raised in those religions, but I think they see it as sort of a church membership thing or maybe something that helps the baby go to Heaven in the case that it dies."

"Does it?"

"Babies are innocent. They can't determine good from evil yet. They have no law to follow. I think they'd automatically go to Heaven because the Bible says that *where there is no law, there is no transgression* and that *sin is not imputed when there is no law*. Babies have no law to be held accountable for, and no understanding of such things. Do you understand?"

"I think so. So, why did the people get baptized in the Bible?"

"It signifies two things. It is a public profession of your faith. It shows the world that you are a Christian. You're identifying yourself with Christ. And it is a step of obedience. Even Christ was baptized as an example for us to follow."

"Oh." She stared at her drink as though deep in thought. "So, should *I* be baptized then? Were *you* baptized?"

"Yep. I got baptized when I was seven, right after I accepted Christ as my Saviour."

"Where do they do it?"

"I was baptized in a river, but that's not necessary. It can be a swimming pool, a baptismal, anything that has a lot of water. Notice what we read, how they went *down into* the water. They weren't just sprinkled. When Jesus saves you, he saves *all* of you. My theory is that is why they were fully submerged in the Biblical examples. Because Christ cleanses us thoroughly, totally."

She shrugged. "It makes sense to me. Will you baptize me?"

"Me?" He chuckled. "I've never baptized anyone before. I can talk to the pastor about it, if you'd like."

"Okay." She smiled.

He loved the enthusiasm and eagerness she exuded. He wished she'd be around longer so he could have a chance to disciple her. There was no doubt she'd have a hundred and one questions and he wanted to be able to help her find the answers.

She shivered slightly.

"Are you cold?" He took off his coat and wrapped it around her, pulling her near in the process. He longed to kiss her, but he wouldn't. Nevertheless, the temptation remained.

"Thank you." Her cheeks sported pink blotches, most likely from the cold. "The temperature really dropped since this afternoon."

"Yes, but no snow." He frowned.

"Nope. We don't get any here. But you could drive up to the mountains. There's snow up there in the higher elevations."

The cold began seeping in through his shirt. "Let's start walking. I need to get the circulation going." He sipped his cider, hoping it would warm him.

"Okay. We can start walking back to the house."

"That sounds good."

Ten minutes later, they entered Samantha's home. Everything seemed quiet with the exception of the fireplace crackling. The Christmas tree stood in a corner, brightly decorated with ornaments and colorful lights that twinkled off and on periodically. There were no longer gifts underneath tree.

"I think everyone has gone to bed," Samantha whispered. "We can sit in the living room. I'll get us more cider. Go ahead and have a seat on the couch."

William stepped near the fireplace to warm his hands, then did as his host suggested. He didn't look forward to the walk back to the Marshall residence.

As a matter of fact, he'd probably jog back.

He heard voices echoing from the kitchen. Apparently, her father had awakened. A buttery aroma filled the air and William's mouth began to water as he anticipated his first handful of popcorn.

True to her word, Samantha appeared in the living room with two mugs of steaming cider. A large bowl was nestled between her arm and abdomen and he quickly offered to relieve her of it.

"Mm...popcorn. This smells delicious." He popped some into his mouth.

Samantha plopped down next to him on the couch, her face glowing in the firelight. "I love popcorn."

"Was that your dad you were talking to?"

"Yes. He told me to lock up after you leave and my mother wanted to invite you over for breakfast in the morning."

"That sounds great. What time?"

"Probably about seven. Dad's got to be to work at eight."

"I look forward to it."

Samantha snuggled closer and he draped his arm around her. He could imagine spending the rest of his life like this. Just the two of them on a quiet evening, enjoying quiet conversation and a snack by the fire. It almost seemed like it wasn't real, like he was dreaming or living somebody else's life or watching a movie.

"This is really nice." He voiced his thoughts.

"It is, isn't it? I'm going to miss you when I'm gone."

He brushed his lips against her hair. She felt so good in his arms. "I'll miss you more."

She laughed. "I seriously doubt that. You'll have all those young people to keep you occupied. Lonely ol' me will be off at college all by myself, away from everyone."

He sipped his cider. "You forget that I'm away from my family and friends too."

Samantha frowned and a reflection of the fire burned in her eyes. "Let's not talk about that right now. Let's talk about when I get back."

William shook his head. "One day at a time. You're not gone yet. What are we going to do while you're *here*?"

"Well, since I flew home on a whim, I have no plans. My schedule is pretty much wide open."

"You don't have any friends you want to catch up with?"

"Nah, not really. I'm closest to Emily and she didn't come home for Christmas break." Samantha moved closer to him. "We could take a walk around town tomorrow."

"I'd love that. You can show me all around."

Samantha laughed. "There's not that much to see, but okay."

She looked up and he couldn't resist a small kiss with her face so near to his. He longed to take her face in his hands, but didn't want to smear butter on her cheeks. Maybe it was better that way.

William sighed in contentment. Did she realize what she did to him inside? How he longed to make her his wife? "I don't want this to end."

"Neither do I."

But it was way too soon to ask her to make a lifelong commitment to him. Could a man even know that he wanted to spend the rest of his life with someone he'd only met just days ago? Perhaps he should take a step back so he could think clearly. She had college to finish and he had his job, not that he couldn't manage a wife and his pastorate. He needed time to adjust though.

CHAPTER EIGHT

"Okay, it's your last night here. What do you want to do?" William warmed his hands against the vehicle's heater and smiled at Samantha.

"Spend time with you." She looked adorable in her beanie and scarf, all bundled up.

"Is there any place to ice skate out here?" He thought it silly to even be asking, since it wasn't even freezing outside.

"I think so. I'm pretty sure they opened up an outdoor ice skating rink in downtown Fresno."

"Really?" He pulled out his cell phone and searched the internet. "I found it. Would you like to go?"

"If you can hold my hand and show me how, I'm up for anything."

"You've *never* been ice skating?"

Samantha shook her head. "Not really. I mean, I did try once for a few minutes at an indoor rink at a friend's birthday party when I was ten. I'm not sure if that counts." She shrugged.

"It looks like it's time for you to learn then." He grinned.

———— ❧ ————

William unlaced his ice skates as he sat on the bench next to Samantha. "I don't know about you, but I could really use a cup of hot cocoa right about now."

"That sounds good." She reached over and clasped his hand. "Thanks for bringing me, William. It was a lot of fun."

"Even though that little boy knocked you down?" He reached for her ice skates.

"I'll probably have a sore bottom, but I'll be all right. What matters is having you by my side."

William reached for her hair and caressed her face. "I feel the same way. Come on, let's go warm up."

His heart did a flip at the thought of someday taking Samantha home with him. He'd love to take her to his family's farm where he'd grown up, to the pond on their property that he'd learned to ice skate on as a young boy.

"What are you thinking?" Samantha's questioning gaze met his.

He winked. "About our future."

"I like the sound of that. Our future." She stood on her tiptoes and kissed his cheek.

———— ❧ ————

Samantha's departure had been bittersweet. He didn't want to see her go, yet she had to in order for him to set his plan into motion. If he were to make a surprise visit for her birthday in the spring, he'd need to find a way to make that happen.

And that would require finding an extra source of income. First, he'd talk to Pastor Marshall to see if he'd heard about any local job openings. Next, he'd put in his application and pray that he got hired. A job would do him good. It would give him a chance to meet local folks outside the church, and it would keep his mind occupied while Samantha was away.

CHAPTER NINE

William looked at the group of young people around him as they lounged on couches, recliners, bean bags, and miscellaneous folding chairs. Some even sat on the floor. He really appreciated the laid back atmosphere and felt like it took pressure off him and the teens. "So, is everyone excited to be back in school and start the new year?"

He heard a collective groan from the group and chuckled. "Hey, I've been where you are. Trust me, it'll go by a lot faster than you think."

One of the young men raised his hand. "I know what you mean, Pastor. It seems like I just barely started high school and now I'm in my senior year, about to graduate in a few months."

William nodded. "What are you planning to do after that, Josh?"

"I'm not sure. My parents want me to go to college."

"And how do you feel about that?"

He shrugged. "I don't really know."

"Do you have any plans? What are your goals?" William challenged.

"I guess I don't really have any." Josh blew out a breath.

"Well, what do you want to do with your life? Is there anything you're interested in?"

"I'd like to see the world."

William nodded. "Maybe you could study overseas?"

"That might be cool."

Another teen boy spoke up. "What about you, Pastor? Why did you choose *this* job? Wouldn't you rather be a policeman or a soldier or a firefighter? You know, have a hero's job? Make all the ladies *swoon* after you." He placed the back of his hand on his forehead.

The small crowd chuckled at the last comment and the boy's physical illustration of it.

William smiled. "That's a great question, Mason. I guess I could have chosen one of those professions. And you're right, they are very noble jobs. But I'd like to think that trying to snatch people from an eternity in Hell *is* a hero's job, a noble profession."

The teens looked at one another, nodding their heads as they pondered William's words.

William surveyed the group. "Anyone else have any dreams or know what they'd like to do in the future?"

A girl raised her hand.

"Yes, Sarah?"

She smiled timidly. "I enjoy sewing."

William nodded. "That's a talent not too many people possess nowadays. What do you like to make?"

"Just whatever. I love to find new patterns. It's challenging."

"There's a lot you can do with sewing."

She leaned forward on the couch she was sitting on, between two of her friends. "Like what?"

"Well, there's the wedding industry. You could make bridal gowns, dresses, the sky's the limit." He smiled. "There's also theater and movie wardrobe. Or if you enjoy teaching, you could do that as well."

William could just read the excitement on her face as she thought of all the possibilities.

"What about me?" Another young lady—who looked to be a few months away from giving birth—

asked. "I won't be able to do much of anything."

"Tawny, being a mother and raising children to honor and respect others and to follow God, is the noblest profession anyone can have. Don't let anyone ever tell you differently."

"Can God still use me, even though I've messed up?" The thread of hope in her tone didn't escape William's notice.

"You bet He can." He pointed to the Bible on the podium. "The Bible is full of stories of imperfect people who God used to do extraordinary things."

"Like who?"

"Have you ever heard of Solomon?"

One of the boys volunteered. "He was supposed to be the wisest man that ever lived, right?"

"That's right." He surveyed the group. "Can anyone tell me who his mother was?"

The same young man raised his hand. "Was it Bathsheba?"

"That's right. The mother of the wisest man was a woman who'd had an affair." William nodded. "And not only was she the mother of Solomon, she was also part of the lineage of Christ."

"Why do you suppose that is, Pastor? Why would God use someone like that?"

William smiled. "We're all imperfect, Ethan. Every single one of us. If God waited to find a perfect person to work through, nothing would ever get done. And I think He wants us to have hope. He wants us to know that no matter how far down we sink, He can always redeem us. But our lives will be far easier if we do things His way in the first place. Every sin has a consequence."

"Thanks for moving here, Pastor William. I like you. You're cool." Ethan grinned.

"Well, I am from Ohio. We do get snow there." William chuckled but nobody laughed. "You know, cool—snow. Never mind. Seriously, though, I'm glad I moved too. And not just because of my girlfriend. I enjoy hanging out with you guys."

CHAPTER TEN

William tapped the envelope in his hand as Mrs. Marshall queried him about his plans. All he could think of was getting to his room and savoring every word of Samantha's letter.

"How is the grocery store working out for you, William? Are you enjoying working there?" Her rosy cheeks reflected her equally rosy personality.

"It's going well, Mrs. Marshall. Lifting those boxes of inventory is just as worthwhile as going to the gym. And I get paid." William smiled.

"Will you be joining us for dinner this evening or do you work tonight?"

"I do work, but not until eight. And dinner sounds wonderful. Let me know if you need anything while I'm at the store. You have my phone number on the refrigerator."

"I will, William. You're such a kind and thoughtful young man."

"Thank you, ma'am."

As soon as Pastor Marshall's wife disappeared from the hallway, William made a beeline to his bedroom. Being allowed to live with the Marshalls rent-free had truly been a blessing. He would eventually need to find a place of his own, especially if he intended on marrying Samantha in the future. He'd had no idea how expensive renting a place out here would be. It seemed almost double to what a comparable place would have rented for in Ohio. As it was, his church salary would barely cover rent. He'd definitely need a decent paying second job if he had in mind to provide for a family.

He removed his jacket and tossed it on the bed, then quickly planted himself in the office chair that accompanied the small desk in his room. He pulled out Samantha's letter.

Dear William,

I hope this letter finds you well. School is going okay, but I miss you a lot and find myself thinking of you often. Are you still enjoying working with the kids at church? Has anything new or exciting happened lately? I know that Kingsburg isn't the most exciting town there is, but I'm guessing you enjoy that-being from Ohio.

The weather here is still cold. It snowed yesterday. I stayed home because of sickness last week so now I'm trying to catch up in all my classes. It stinks.

Anyway, you'll be happy to know I've been reading my Bible. I'm really enjoying learning all about God. I do have a couple of questions but I'll ask them next time we talk on the phone, okay?

I really like writing letters instead of texting. It makes it more romantic somehow, plus I get to keep your letters and hide them in a treasure box for our great-grandchildren to read. Ha! Ha! I don't even have a treasure box. Maybe I'll have to find one.

Well, as much as I hate to, I'd better get back to my studies. I can't wait to see *you again! Summer can't come soon enough.*

I love you with all my heart, babe.

Samantha

William folded the letter closed after rereading it and tucked it into his desk drawer with the others. He was hoping to show up for her birthday as a surprise, so he hadn't told Samantha about his second job at the grocery store to earn extra money.

———— ❧ ————

He stared down at his bank statement and grinned. Finally, he'd met his goal. Now, it was only a matter of time until he hopped on a plane and headed east to see the love of his life.

CHAPTER ELEVEN

The last time William was here at the mall, he had no idea he'd be back so soon—*and* making his own special purchase.

"Have you decided which ring you'd like to purchase?" The jeweler smiled in anticipation.

"I can't decide. Which one do you like better? The round or the square?"

"Well, the round cut is certainly the most popular and accounts for approximately seventy-five percent of all diamonds sold. The princess cut, however, has become a popular choice as well—although it's a newer style."

William stared at the two rings. "You know what? I think I'll go with the round cut. The princess cut is nice, but it seems like it might get caught on things easier."

"Good choice. You can't go wrong with a classic." The jeweler grasped the velvet box from inside the glass case. "If you need to have it sized or cleaned, just bring it back to us. Both of those are free services we offer with every purchase."

"Do you have a return policy? In case she says no?" William pulled out his bank card and swiped it after the jeweler had given him the total.

"You have sixty days to return the ring, but I hope the next time I see you it'll be to purchase a matching band."

William blew out a breath and grinned. "You and me both."

"Thank you very much, sir." The jeweler handed William a small thick plastic bag with the store logo on it.

William tucked the bag into his interior jacket pocket. "Thank you. Have a great day." He took a Gospel tract out of his pocket and handed it to the jeweler. "Please read this when you get a chance. It will explain how to get to Heaven."

The man nodded, then eyed him somewhat suspiciously.

William left the store with a smile and offered a prayer for the jeweler's salvation.

Now, to stop by Samantha's folks' place. At just the thought, his hands already began perspiring.

———&~———

William knocked on the door and briefly thought of turning and running in the other direction. *Please give me courage, Lord.*

The door swung open. "William, what brings you by today?" Samantha's father's chipper greeting set him at ease. That was a good sign, right?

William attempted to swallow down the lump in his throat. "Mr. Hanson, may I have a word with you, please?"

The gentleman's brow rose. No doubt, curious about William's visit. "Sure, come on in." He opened the door for William to enter. "Would you like a glass of lemonade?"

"That would be a blessing, thank you." William nodded and followed his host.

"You may have a seat at the table, if you'd like." Mr. Hanson gestured to the breakfast nook and stepped into the kitchen. He removed two glasses from the cupboard and filled them. "This warmer weather has been nice, hasn't it?"

"Yes, sir, it has." William took his cue and sat

down. He waited until Samantha's father sat down as well.

It would be best if he just came out with it before he lost his nerve. "Sir, I won't beat around the bush or waste your time. The truth is, I'm in love with your daughter, Samantha. The reason I'm here is I'd like to ask your permission to marry her."

Mr. Hanson's brow furrowed. "Wait. You want permission? From *me*?"

"Yes, sir."

"Well, that's awfully thoughtful of you, William. I was unaware that young men still did that sort of thing in this day and age."

"I think marriages do better if couples have the blessing and support of their loved ones."

He shrugged. "Well, personally, I think it's a matter between you and my daughter. That would be her decision to make."

"So, you don't have any objections? Questions or concerns maybe?" William played with the condensation on his glass.

"How long have you and my daughter known each other?"

William swallowed. "About three and a half months."

Samantha's father frowned. "That's not very long."

"I realize that, sir. I plan to wait until Christmas before we actually marry."

"And you think a year is a long enough time for you and my daughter to get to know each other?"

"Yes, sir. I do. Marriages have thrived with far less time. The senior pastor at my former church met and married his wife in two months' time. They've been married for almost fifty years now." William took a sip of his lemonade. "I believe that marriage is a lifetime commitment and I don't consider divorce to be an option. We would attend marriage counseling prior to the wedding."

Mr. Hanson rubbed the slightly greying stubble on his chin. "You're a pastor, right? Do pastors even make enough money to support a family?"

William grimaced. "I'm a youth pastor. My pay is certainly not the most desirable, but as the head of the house, I do plan to provide. This will be my responsibility to your daughter and any family we might have. The Bible says that the man who doesn't provide for his own is worse than an infidel. I have no intention of letting my family go without. If my pastoring job isn't sufficient, I'll seek extracurricular employment."

Mr. Hanson nodded. "You're from...where?"

"Ohio."

"You're not planning to marry my daughter then cart her off to Ohio, are you?"

"The Lord has called me to serve in Kingsburg, and this is where I plan to stay unless the Lord directs me elsewhere. And that would be a decision your daughter and I would make together."

"Have you and my daughter discussed this yet?"

"Marriage? Ah, no. Not yet."

"But you think she'll say yes?"

"I sure hope so. That's what I've been praying for." William smiled.

Mr. Hanson's demeanor turned serious. "What if I said I'd like you to wait another year?"

"Then I would honor your wishes, sir. Although I admit it would be difficult."

"Congratulations, William." Samantha's father reached out his hand and William shook it. "You have my blessing." He smiled.

William was slightly confused. "*Now*, or in a year?"

He chuckled. "You may ask her now, but I ask that you would honor your word and marry no sooner than December."

"Thank you very much, sir!"

"If you're going to marry my daughter, we're probably going to have to come up with a different name for you to call me. Sir is too formal. How about Tom?"

"Tom it is." William smiled.

"I've got to admit, this was a surprise. But it's a pleasant surprise. Do you know how we found out about my other daughter's proposal?"

"No, sir. Uh, Tom, I mean."

"Well, let's just say it went something like this. 'Daddy, Travis and I are getting married. By the way, we're expecting a baby too.' I much prefer the way you're going about it."

"I can imagine. Although none of us is perfect. I'm far from it." William met his gaze. "For the record, I'm planning to wait until marriage."

"Thank you, William. The level of respect I've seen of you is refreshing and admirable."

"I appreciate you saying that. Thank you, Tom. I don't want to take up any more of your time." He rose from the table and took his empty glass to the sink.

"Why don't you join us for a meal this week? It's just my wife and me now that Jaime's married,

Samantha's in college, and Scott moved back up north."

"That's a kind offer. I accept."

"Will Thursday at six thirty work for you?"

"Thursday will be perfect. See you then."

CHAPTER TWELVE

The flight had taken entirely too long for William's taste. Seeing Samantha after being separated for three months would equate to a wonderful fantasy. He hoped she'd feel the same way when he knocked on her door and surprised her.

He maneuvered the rental car and parked near the curb of the apartment complex she resided in. Taking a deep breath, he grabbed hold of the bouquet of flowers he'd purchased at a nearby grocery store.

William glanced at his guitar. It had been a pain to have to check it in at the airport, but he wanted to have it with him. He thought of the song he'd written for her—for them. What would she think when he sang it for her tonight? Just before proposing to her.

He pondered the words and hummed the song. Should he practice one more time? He put the flowers down and moved his seat back. He opened his guitar case and pulled out the sheet music.

His Will

I'd never known love until He came along and showed me His love, showed me His will for me.

His will for me was love. His will for me was love.

I'd never known joy until He came along and showed me His joy, showed me His will for me.

His will for me was joy. His will for me was joy.

I'd never known peace until He came along and showed me His peace, showed me His will for me.

His will for me was peace. His will for me was peace.

I'd never known you until He came along and showed me His love, showed me His will for me.

His will for me was you. His will for us was love.

We'd never known love until He came along and showed us His love, showed me His will for us.

We'd never known love until He came along and showed us His love, showed me His will for us.

I'd never known love until He came along and showed me His love, showed me His will...

He second guessed himself once again. He'd felt so inspired when he wrote it, but now? Was this even good enough to sing for Samantha? *Just do it*, he told himself. *For God hath not given us the spirit of fear.*

Somehow, he gathered his nerve and finally exited the vehicle. As he walked past apartment doors, he carefully read each number.

There it was.

He knocked.

No answer.

Oh shoot, she's not home. He hadn't contemplated this scenario. Perhaps he should go to his hotel room and return later. He pondered what his next step should be.

"May I help you?" A voice called from behind him. He turned around.

A young man near his own age stared at the bouquet in his hands. "Looking for Samantha? They went out for her birthday."

"Do you know where?"

"I think they said they were going to The Buckle."

"The Buckle?"

"Yes, the country bar and grill on Second Street."

"Second Street. Okay, thank you." William briefly thought about telling the guy not to mention that he'd stopped by, in case Samantha returned before he found her and they missed each other.

He typed 'The Buckle' into his phone's GPS and soon found the driving directions. A few minutes later, he stopped in The Buckle's parking lot and decided to leave the flowers in the car. Music poured out of the building.

William frowned. He didn't care much for noisy places.

But it didn't matter tonight. All that mattered was seeing the girl of his dreams and giving her what he hoped would be her best birthday surprise ever. He patted the pocket inside his jacket just to make sure the precious contents still resided within.

He hadn't expected to be nervous but with each step he took, it seemed his anxiety cranked up a notch. He pushed the door open and was greeted by a hostess wearing a little less than she should.

"Table for one?"

He diverted his gaze. "Uh, no. I'm meeting a friend. I'll just hang out here until I find her, if that's all right."

"Sure thing, sugar." She disappeared behind a counter and took a set of menus to a nearby table.

William eyed each patron in search of Samantha. The smoke-filled room didn't make it easy. The live band started up again, playing some sort of country song and he turned his attention to the dancefloor.

He smiled. There she was, just beyond it.

He allowed himself to drink in the sight of her— only for a moment or two. He noticed her dark blue denim jacket, her pink floral dress that fit her just right, her cowboy boots. Her face beamed as she chatted, surrounded by her friends. Everything about this young woman was beautiful—her long brown hair, her striking eyes, her gorgeous smile. And the thought of spending the rest of his life with her, thrilled him to the core. If all went as planned, this wonderful woman would become his fiancée tonight. What a night it would be!

He began walking in that general direction, then stopped dead in his tracks. What was Samantha doing in the arms of another man? He stood in place, as though his shoes were superglued to the floor, and stared shamelessly as this cowboy swayed to the slow music with *his* girl.

He wanted to rush over there and give the guy a piece of his mind, or maybe his fist. His heart raced with fury and he stepped forward, his hands clenched at his sides. This couldn't end well.

You're a pastor. You cannot walk into a bar and start a fight, he told himself. *Just walk away.*

He'd all but lost it when the cowboy leaned close and met her lips with his. *No!*

Walk away. William couldn't watch any more. So he turned around and did one of the most difficult things he'd ever done in his life—he walked away, bolted for the exit. He couldn't get out of that place fast enough.

William headed back to his hotel room, practically screeching around every corner. He abruptly stopped at the red signal, drumming on the steering wheel. The light illuminated the bouquet of flowers that sat in his front seat. He felt like chucking them out the window or into a garbage can.

Instead, he turned and headed back to Samantha's apartment. He walked to her door and sat the flowers on the ground. If she found them, fine. If someone else found them, fine. It really didn't matter at this point. All he knew was he couldn't stand to look at them anymore.

He glanced down at the small card that accompanied the flowers.

Happy Birthday, to the girl of my dreams.
Love, William

Pain cinched down on his heart.

He decided to leave the card with the flowers.

Samantha had to at least know how he felt. She had to know that she was the most important person in the world to him. She had to know the devotion she'd given up.

———— ❧ ————

Why, Lord?

William sat in his hotel room, his face buried in his hands.

What he had witnessed less than an hour ago had to be the most painful thing he'd ever felt. How could Samantha do that to him? When did she plan to tell him that she was seeing someone else?

Here, he'd spent months working and saving up money to fly halfway across the country. For what? For this? It didn't seem fair.

He thought of his friend Marcus. He'd been right all along.

He had been a fool to think somehow it would be different with him and Samantha. He should have never given his heart away.

CHAPTER THIRTEEN

William stared aimlessly at the wall in his office. It had been over a month since his surprise visit. Since the incident. Since his world had come crashing down.

He looked down at the letter that had arrived yesterday. It was the second one he'd received since he'd returned to Kingsburg. The first one had been written in the same vein as Samantha's other letters to him—she'd thanked him for the birthday flowers and said how much she missed him. *Yeah, right.*

This letter took on a whole different persona.

Dear William,

I don't know what to say. I've written you and tried to call and even text, but you seem to be ignoring me. Why?

I'm guessing that you no longer wish to continue our relationship. That's fine. But ending it without a reason or without confronting me is cowardice. I thought you were better than that. I guess I was wrong.

I thought we had something special. I thought you were different than all the other guys out there. I guess I was wrong about that too.

Goodbye,
Samantha

He didn't get it. Not at all. She acted as though she were innocent in this whole matter. *She* cheated on *him*!

He felt like tearing up the letter and tossing it into the garbage can.

A knock on the door stole his attention and brought him back to earth. "Come in."

Brother Jackson, one of the deacons, popped his head in. "William, you're still on for working the booth at the Swedish Festival next weekend, right?"

"I'll be there." His smile felt flat.

"Hey, you doin' all right? Everything okay?"

William heard the concern in Brother Jackson's tone.

"Yeah, I'll survive. Just goin' through a rough patch right now."

He stepped into the office. "May I pray for you?"

"I'd appreciate that, Brother." They both bowed their heads in prayer.

Even though moving here had been quite an adjustment, he knew this was where God wanted him to be. He loved his church family and he enjoyed working with the youth.

If Samantha moved back and stayed here permanently, it would no doubt be a challenge. He could only avoid her for so long. It would be no time at all until they bumped into each other, especially with him working at the local grocery store. He usually stocked shelves and worked on inventory, but occasionally they'd ask him to man one of the cash registers.

What would happen if Samantha were a customer? Would they talk to each other with pleasantries? Would they give each other the silent treatment? Would they erupt into an argument in front of other customers and his coworkers? Would he lose his job?

That wouldn't be good—it wouldn't be good at all.

CHAPTER FOURTEEN

William glanced down at his study notes.

The Pitfalls of Relationships.

He'd mulled over it several times.

Note to self: NEVER invest in a romantic long-distance relationship!!!!!

Not that he needed to write it down to remember it. No, excruciating heartbreaks like that had no need of a reminder. Why would it, when it was at the forefront of his mind? Every. Single. Day.

Did Samantha have any idea what she'd done to him? Over a month later and he still felt like his heart had been ripped out, shredded to teeny tiny pieces, currently on life support, and barely beating. Why did loving so hard, so intensely, have to hurt so much?

He opened his desk drawer and stared at the

engagement ring he'd purchased for her. He couldn't force himself to return it to the jewelers, so there it sat. A daily reminder of lost love. Maybe he should put it on Craig's List. He knew he'd only get a fraction of what he paid for it, but then he wouldn't have to think about her rejection.

Who was he kidding? He'd think about Samantha whether the ring was present or not. How could he ever get over losing her? How could he tell his heart to beat again, when all it wanted to do was bury itself in sorrow? Salve would not heal this wound. Surgery would not heal this wound. But deep inside he knew, although at the moment it was difficult to believe, that the Saviour could heal this wound.

God, please help me. I can't do this anymore.

His head jerked up at the knock on his office door. "It's open."

The church secretary, Mrs. Johnson, lifted a half smile. "There's a certain young lady asking to see you."

He sighed. "Tell Jenna not right now. She can text me or talk to me at church or youth group."

"It's not Jenna." Her eyes zeroed in on his. "It's your ex-girlfriend."

William frowned. "Samantha?"

Mrs. Johnson nodded.

"Please tell her I'm not available."

"Are you sure? She's called the church office several times over the last—"

"Please tell her I'm not available." He had to stand his ground. He couldn't bear to see Samantha. To look her in the eye.

"Very well, then."

William blew out a breath as the secretary turned and walked back to the reception area.

Why was Samantha even here? He was surprised she didn't stay in town with Mr. Rodeo—or maybe he'd merely been a college fling? Anger surged through his veins at just the thought of seeing her in the cowboy's arms. Would he ever get that image out of his mind?

The door to his office suddenly burst open. "I want to know why you stopped writing to me. Why didn't you answer any of my letters?" Samantha demanded with arms crossed over her chest.

William's mouth hung open. He hastily moved to his office door and stuck his head out. Mrs. Johnson held up both of her hands and shrugged. He sighed and closed the door to what would certainly be a loud exchange.

He faced her. "I thought that would be obvious. You're not the girl I thought you to be."

Was that remorse on her face? And so it should be. Maybe she finally realized what she'd given up. "I'm sorry. I can't change the past. Listen, William. I know I should have been honest with you from the start. I just thought that if you knew that Travis and I slept together, you'd react this way."

"You *slept* with him *too*?!" *That jerk.* He dug both hands into his hair, shaking his head in disbelief. His heart plunged even lower. Why was she telling him this? He didn't want the details!

"What do you mean, 'too'? I thought that was what we were discussing?"

"I should have listened to my conscience. It was a mistake to ever agree to a long-distance relationship. I knew it would never work. We'd only been apart a few months and you're not only dating, but have also been intimate with another guy. Samantha, I thought I could trust you. I wrote you. I told you that I loved you. I guess all that wasn't enough."

"What are you talking about? What happened with Travis and me was two years ago."

"Two years ago?" William scratched his head and frowned. "I'm confused."

"Not as confused as I am."

He thrust his hands into his pockets. "Who's Travis?"

"Travis was my ex-boyfriend who's now married to my sister."

"And he came to your college?"

"What? You're totally confusing me. No. I *only* dated Travis in high school. He broke up with me and that's *why* I went off to college."

"I don't understand what's going on."

"All I know is *you* stopped writing to me and I wanted to find out why. I thought maybe you'd started seeing someone else." Her lip began quivering.

"Seeing someone el—?" His brow lowered. "No! *I* have not been the one seeing someone else."

"What's that supposed to mean? Are you implying that *I* have?"

"No, I'm not *implying* anything. I'm stating a simple fact."

"I don't know what you mean."

"You don't know what I mean?" He nodded and sighed. It figured she would deny it. "Seriously, Samantha? I already know the truth. Don't lie about it; I hate lying. Just admit that you've been seeing another guy!" He clenched his hands tightly at his sides. He felt like throwing something, but he wouldn't let his temper get the best of him.

She stared at him blankly.

"Let me refresh your memory. A bar. A dance. A kiss. Your birthday." He really didn't want to go there. Again.

"Jill and Tammy took me out to the grill for my birth—" Samantha's eyes bulged. "Wait a minute! You think that I was seeing Jace Armstrong?" She shook her head. "I'm not, nor have I *ever* been interested in Jace. Yes, I danced with him—out of kindness and nothing else. Yes, he kissed me—without my permission. It earned him a good kick in the shin." She stared at William. "Wait a minute. How do *you* know about that? Who told you?"

"I saw it with my own two eyes." But he hadn't seen her kick the guy. Was she telling the truth? Could he have misinterpreted the entire event?

"But how did you see it? Did someone post a video on Facebook?"

"I wanted to surprise you on your birthday. But it turned out, the surprise was on me." He grimaced.

"You were there? You came to see me on my birthday?" She sounded touched, but he was still having a hard time believing her story. But if it was true...

He nodded. "I took a second job at the grocery store so I could earn extra money to come see you. I had this wonderful evening planned for us." He thought about the romantic dinner he'd made reservations for. The song he'd written and wanted to sing for her. The ring he'd anticipated giving her. Reliving his dashed hopes again was hard.

"I got the flowers, but... I-I don't know what to say, William. Here, I thought that *you* were seeing someone else...and you thought..." She frowned. "No wonder you never wrote back to me. I feel terrible. I'm so sorry about this whole mess."

"Yeah. Me too. I was furious when I left to come back home. I said some things that needed to be repented of," he admitted. "I even took some time off work." He sighed.

"Can we just do this over? Please?"

"I don't want to do it over. The first time around was awful enough."

"I meant *differently* this time."

"I know. I was teasing." It felt so good to smile again. "Listen, Samantha. About Travis...when we met, I never expected you to be perfect. We all make mistakes we have to live with. There's nothing we can do to change the past."

"You forgive me?"

"Of course. I just wish…" He walked around to the other side of his desk and opened the top drawer. He handed her the small wrapped gift box that held the ring. "This was supposed to be your birthday present."

She stared at him in astonishment.

"Please, open it." He'd chosen a bigger box than a typical ring box on purpose to wrap it in. He didn't want her to guess it was a ring.

She gingerly unwrapped the box, then stared down at the ring. "William?"

"I wasn't sure of the size. I hope it fits." He was bumbling. *Just get to the point.* "I was going to ask…I mean, if you wanted to…" He raked a hand through his hair. "Sheesh, I'm so clumsy at this, it's not even funny."

She waited patiently for him to get the words out.

"Will you marry me, Samantha? *Please*?" He swallowed. "I was hoping we could be married by next Christmas. *This* Christmas, I mean. I'd like to take you home to meet my folks. I already talked to your father and he was okay with it."

"You went and talked to my father?" Her jaw dropped ever so slightly.

He nodded, awaiting her answer.

"Yes." She bit her bottom lip. "And December's perfect."

"Yes? For real? You'll marry me?"

She had tears in her eyes. That had to be a good thing, right? "Yes, William. I'll marry you."

"Oh no, I should have gotten down on one knee." He mentally chastised himself.

"It doesn't matter."

He slipped the diamond ring onto her finger, loving the smile that accompanied it.

This time, he took her into his arms and lowered his lips to hers. It was a sweet slow kiss that expressed the joy his heart was feeling. A joy he thought he'd never know again. "I love you, Samantha."

"I love you too," she murmured.

He pulled back and gazed into her eyes. "Please, don't ever dance with another guy again."

"I won't. I promise. Unless it's my dad or brother."

William grinned. "I think that would be acceptable."

He went to his office door, opened it, and stuck his head out. "Attention, everybody! I just asked Samantha to marry me and she said yes!" he proclaimed in the hallway of the church administration building.

One by one, they received congratulations and well wishes from all who were present.

Today had gone nothing like he'd planned, but that was a wonderful thing. Wonderful indeed!

CHAPTER FIFTEEN

William stood at the front of the church, feeling a little silly in his jeans, as Samantha walked slowly toward him. Her smile no doubt gleamed as bright as his own.

Tomorrow was the day!

They'd marry in the morning on the twenty-third, then fly out to Ohio to spend Christmas with his family. He could barely contain his excitement as he thought about introducing Samantha to his family, taking her for a walk on their property and showing her all his favorite spots, ice skating with her on the pond that he learned had been frozen over for a couple of weeks now, cuddling with her by the hearth that had always loomed large in his folks' home.

And of course, he looked forward to their

wedding night. He'd called ahead and arranged everything with his mother. The detached garage, turned into spare guest quarters, would be ready and waiting, just the way he'd planned. Chocolate truffles on the pillows with a chilled bottle of non-alcoholic wine on the night stand next to the bed. On the other night stand would be a large bouquet of red roses with a very special note for his wife's eyes only. Red rose petals on the comforter and the carpet. Scented candles around the Jacuzzi tub. A blazing faux fire in the electric heater.

And then they would continue their honeymoon—touring the lighthouses of the Eastern Coastline. *It'll be absolutely perfect!*

Samantha joined him at the altar as they went through the preparations for what would take place tomorrow.

"You ready to do this, my love?" He took her hands in his.

She smiled and nodded. "More than ready."

The look of love and adoration in her eyes was more than he could hope for.

"What are you thinking?" she asked.

"I'm thinking that making Samantha Marie Hanson my wife will be the most wonderful thing

I've done in my life after accepting Christ." He winked.

She smiled. "I feel exactly the same way."

EPILOGUE

William reached for his wife's hand and drew her closer to him. Soon, they'd be arriving back in the California Central Valley, ready to move into their own place and begin their new life together. "Do you remember the first time we were on an airplane together?"

He read the love in her eyes as she leaned over and kissed his lips. "I'll never forget that day."

"That makes two of us. You know, I thought about *this* day then."

"Really?" She lightly caressed his arm.

"Well, kind of." He smiled. "I'd glanced at your hand to see if you were married."

Her smile grew wide. "You're kidding me."

He shook his head. "And I thought about kissing you."

She gasped. "William Harper! You did not."

"I blame it entirely on the Bible."

Samantha laughed out loud.

"What? You don't believe me, Mrs. Harper?" He pulled his Bible out of his carry-on.

"Not for a second." She leaned forward and kissed him again.

He turned to the Song of Solomon. "So here I was, trying to mind my own business—which is not very easy to do when a gorgeous girl is sitting next to you, mind you—and so I pulled out my Bible for a distraction. When I opened it up, I kid you not, this is the verse my eyes landed on." He handed the Bible to her and pointed.

"No way." Her mouth dropped open. She read the words, "*Let him kiss me with the kisses of his mouth, for thy love is better than wine.* Mm...and so it is."

William nodded, a bit distracted at her hand on his chest.

"That sounds...*romantic*. I didn't know *that kind* of stuff was in the Bible."

William laughed. "It gets even more *romantic* than that."

"I had no idea. We'll have to read it later." She

grinned. "So, is that why you started talking to me?"

"No. I saw you crying."

"You did?" She nodded. "Yeah, coming home wasn't easy for me. You know, with what happened with Travis and all. And then, I found out about him and my sister...I'm just so glad I met you, William. Travis would never even be able to hold a candle next to you."

"It was almost like God had whispered to me from the very beginning, *'This is going to be your wife.'* And then, we realized we were headed to the same town and you knew my driver. And then, we saw each other at the mall. It was just too much of a coincidence."

"I know what you mean. I thought you were pretty cute, and nice, but I was a little leery. And when you told me you were a youth pastor, *that* was totally a foreign thing to me. It was almost as if I felt like you lived on another planet or something."

"And now you live on that planet with me." He winked.

"We could live all alone on our own planet and I wouldn't care one bit. I'd just be happy that we were there together." She cupped his face and met him with a kiss. "I love you, Mr. Harper."

He pressed his lips to hers, not caring if other travelers in the airplane noticed their public display of affection. "I love you too, Mrs. Harper."

THE END

Thank you for reading!

If you enjoyed this book, you'll want to sign up for
Michelynn Christy's newsletter.
blessedpublishing1@gmail.com

Other titles by **Michelynn**:
Love Unawares
If He Only Knew
A Groom for Christmas

Other holiday titles available from
Blessed Publishing:

A Christmas of Mercy by J.E.B. Spredemann
Christmas in Paradise by J.E.B. Spredemann

A SPECIAL THANK YOU

I'd like to take this time to thank everyone that had any involvement in this book and its production, including my Mom and Dad, who have always been supportive of my writing, my longsuffering Family - especially my handsome, encouraging Hubby, my supportive Pastor and Church family, my Proofreaders, my Editors, my CIA Facebook friends who have been a tremendous help, my wonderful Readers who buy, read, and leave encouraging reviews and emails.

Last, but certainly not least, I'd like to thank my Precious LORD and SAVIOUR JESUS CHRIST, for without Him, none of this would have been possible!

A sneak peek at Michelynn Christy's
Love Unawares...

ONE

Prairie, Texas 1895

"Well, Jed. Are you ready to meet your new wife tomorrow?" James set his drumstick down, wiped his mouth with his shirt sleeve, and smiled at his brother.

Jedidiah shook his head. "I still don't know about this."

"We're all nervous when we marry." His sister-in-law, Brenda, nodded to his daughter. "Remember, you need to think about little Abilene."

"I know, Brenda." He glanced down at the toddler on his lap and gently kissed her soft flaxen hair. *If only her mother were still alive.* "She's the only reason I agreed to this."

"She looked perty enough in her photograph," his brother mused.

"It ain't that. I just miss Catherine so much. I don't know if I'll make a good husband for any other woman."

"Well, accordin' to Parson John, she comes from a good Christian family. I'm sure ya can learn to love her." Brenda began to clear the dishes from the table.

"No. Not like my Cathy," Jedidiah insisted.

"Well, you just leave that part to the Good Lord, brother." James patted his brother's back.

Jedidiah frowned. "You know how I feel about that subject."

"It wasn't the Lord's fault ya lost Cathy, Jed." His brother's gaze sobered.

"I disagree." Jedidiah's chair screeched as he pushed back from the table. "I better get home. Little Abbie needs her bed." He held his daughter close to his chest.

"You ain't got time for dessert?" His sister-in-law's disappointed look didn't escape his notice. "I made apple pie."

"Can I take a piece home with me?" The last thing Jedidiah wanted to do was miss out on Brenda's delicious apple pie. He lifted his hat from the wall hook and set it on his head.

"Sure. I'll put a slice in for Abbie too." His sister-in-law smiled.

Jed knew she was aware that *he* would be the one to eat both slices. "Thanks, Brenda." He took the pie pan and deposited it in the back of his rig.

"See ya tomorrow, Jed." James waved to him as he drove off in his buckboard.

Jedidiah felt bad about arriving late to the station, but it couldn't be helped. His cow chose this day to deliver her new calf and he had to be present, lest she need help like last time. He'd dropped off Abilene with Brenda this morning and planned to pick her up after stopping at the station. Hopefully, his new bride would be understanding.

"Afternoon, Jed," Timothy Williams, the town hotel's proprietor greeted. "If you're lookin' for a particular young woman, she ain't here."

"What do ya mean?"

"Welp, it just so happens that the stage driver didn't see her when he threw down the luggage. Knocked her clean out."

Jedidiah's eyes widened. "Oh, no."

"You'll find her over in Doc Brown's office."

"Thanks, Tim." Jedidiah set out to find his injured bride.

"By the way, Jed."

He turned around at Timothy's voice. "Ya done real good. She's a right perty thing."

Jedidiah lifted a half-smile and nodded. Being attractive was one thing and certainly didn't hurt, but he knew there were more important traits a wife could possess. His main concern was Abbie's well-being and keepin' the house. If she could handle those two things, he could suffer through whatever other area she may be lacking in. He certainly didn't expect her to be perfect.

He nodded to a few acquaintances in town, then continued on down to the doctor's office near the edge of town. He sighed as he pulled the door open to Doc Brown's office.

"Jedidiah, I hear I have something that belongs to you."

"Someone," Jedidiah clarified. "Where is she?"

"She's lying in my office. I'm afraid she's still out cold."

"May I see her?"

"Sure. Right this way."

Jedidiah followed the doctor from the main

room, down the hall past a couple of doors, and into another smaller room. The old converted house made a perfect office for the doctor. He claimed one room as his own and kept the others vacant for patients in need.

"I'll leave you alone with her. You may speak to her, but don't try to awaken her. It's best if she does that naturally."

"Will she be all right?" He frowned.

"Seems like it."

"Thank ya, Doc." He glanced to where the doctor had just exited the room and was tempted to do the same until he heard a soft moan escape the woman's lips.

Doc Brown's footsteps could be heard down the hallway.

Jedidiah inched toward the bed where his soon-to-be wife lay. He immediately detected an intoxicating floral scent that enveloped her presence. It hadn't necessarily been overwhelming, but her perfume was undeniably noticeable. His gaze unwittingly roamed the gentle curves that graced her fancy lavender dress. He lifted his hand to touch her brow, then hesitated. *What is wrong with me? I shouldn't be thinking on this woman with desire.* He chided himself.

What would Catherine think if she could see him now? He shook his head to dispel his thoughts. If he dwelled on Catherine now, he'd turn around and walk right out for sure.

No, he wouldn't touch her until they were officially married – if he could bring himself to speak the vows. If Ma had taught them anything in their sproutin' up years, it had been to have respect for the female kind. He recalled her words to him and his brother. *"There's already too many rough hands out yonder. I want you boys to make me proud. Do like the Good Book says, 'Do unto others as you want done to you.' If you want a woman to treat you right, then you treat her right."*

Jedidiah frowned. Neither he nor James had found a woman to marry before Ma passed on to Glory. Not even five years later, they'd both found good women. *I hope you're proud now, Ma.* It was a shame Ma never had the chance to meet his sweet Catherine or little Abilene. *Another one of God's curses.* He frowned.

The young woman's soft voice brought his mind back to the present, but he didn't think she'd uttered anything intelligible that would require a response. Her eyes opened slowly and seemed to roam the room taking in her surroundings. She began to rise. Was she even strong enough to sit up?

He cleared his throat. "Uh, Miss. I...I wouldn't be doin' that if I was you."

He sighed when she obediently laid back down.

"Where am I?" Her genteel hand rested on her forehead.

"Prairie, Texas, miss. In Doc Brown's office."

She nodded but confusion permeated her features. "I don't...Are you the doctor?"

He removed his hat and ran a hand through his hair. He was in need of a bath. He'd meant to take one, but was unable to due to tending to the calvin'. He must look a sight.

"No. I—uh." He swallowed. "I'm to be your husband."

Want to read more?

Michelynn's books may be purchased at your favorite online retailer, or requested at your favorite bookstore.